SWEET GRASS SEASON

Sweet Grass Season

J. R. Nakken

IMAGO
PRESS
TUCSON ARIZONA

Published in the United States of America by:

Imago Press
3710 East Edison
Tucson AZ 85716

Names, characters, places, and incidents, unless otherwise specifically noted, are either the product of the author's imagination or are used fictitiously.

LCCN 2009935969

Book and Cover Design by Leila Joiner

ISBN 978-1-935437-07-9
ISBN 1-935437-07-0

Printed in the United States of America on Acid-Free Paper

Acknowledgments

Thanks to readers Kim Gay, Lona Nakken, and N. Liz Crandall. Special thanks to Michael Wolf, who spent a lot of time explaining his black and yellow Omaha dancing regalia to me. And I will be ever grateful to my publisher, Leila Joiner, for fantastic covers and for her continued faith in my work.

Disclaimer

Sweet Grass Season is wholly a work of fiction. The Fort Peck Indian Reservation and the small cities of Poplar, Glasgow, and Wolf Point, Montana are integral components of Eastern Montana, but all descriptions thereof are solely figments of the author's imagination. Any resemblance to persons living or dead is purely coincidental.

For Dale, of course

Chapter One

She didn't see the dark man in the corner, watching her. Tally Carver's exquisite eyes were busy scanning the sparse crowd in the Billings airport. Is this the biggest city in the Big Sky Country of Montana? she wondered. This structure would fit into one corner of Dulles, the airport she had left in civilized Washington, D. C., a few hours ago.

I didn't notice how small it was when I came out to interview, she thought. Oh, well, I'm here. And glad to be anywhere but there! She directed her lithe body toward the baggage claim area, still unaware of the obsidian eyes that followed her progress.

Tally ambled toward the silent steel baggage carousel, hoping to catch sight of someone from the Fort Peck Tribal Office. They were supposed to meet her and deliver her to the as yet sight-unseen apartment on the reservation. But, if all else failed, she knew she could rent a car here at the airport. She had done just that last month, when she flew out to meet with the CEO and Tribal Council for the Tribe's Controller position.

Not yet worried, she quickened her pace as cases and bags began a single file tumble down the shiny slide. Pale, brown hair bounced on the cotton tweed-look sport coat she wore over a white shirt and khaki pants. She looked taller than her 5 feet 6 inches and carried herself like a six-foot runway model. Tally Jo Carver turned the heads of men wearing travel-weary business suits, as well as those in boots and Stetsons, while she walked the concourse.

She's a dandy, thought the dark man at the other end of the building. Wonder if she's mine. He looked at the piece of white cardboard that Ezra Bangs The Drum had sent along with him to Billings. Thalia J. Carver, it read. He shook his head sadly. Probably not.

Joshua Smith's black eyes twinkled as he placed the sign carefully inside the swinging door of a trash receptacle. He strolled toward the silent luggage carousel, his bronze body aimed at the good-looking girl's back.

Tally sensed his gaze, and it wasn't an uncommon feeling. She was unusually perceptive and quite used to being the object of admiring stares. Divorced these three years, she had eased back into the flirtation game reluctantly. She turned now, a half-smile on her face, to acknowledge whoever was behind her.

He was an Indian! Or is it Native American? she wondered. I'll have to ask Mr. Bangs The Drum. I don't want to offend anyone, that's for sure. Well, the handsome whatchacallit guy was eyeballing her!

Tally let her gaze slide past Joshua innocently as she registered his overall appearance. Medium height and broad of chest, he had a dark face and full mouth. She couldn't see his eyes; a battered straw cowboy hat shaded his forehead. Denim sleeves were rolled high on muscular brown arms, and cowboy boots in need of polish showed beneath the well-worn bottoms of his faded Levis. He was a silent sculpture, blue on bronze, watching her.

Tally's heart rate accelerated. She turned her whole body around again, pretended to concentrate on the luggage carousel as it began to rotate. He's just a local native, she thought. Just your first Indian under forty. This is not a real attraction. Don't *do* this, first day in Montana. She took precise mental steps to remove the effect of him from her mind.

The Fort Peck Tribe's newest employee felt the muscular man leave his spot behind her. At the edge of her vision, she marked his disappearance beyond the huge steel chute, now disgorging bags and parcels at a steady clip. She felt suddenly bereft and was momentarily confused at the strength of the emotion.

Joshua formulated a plan as he considered the crowd at the luggage station. It's probably that stone-faced woman in black over there, he decided. This Thalia is some kind of an accounting muckety-muck. Place for everything, everything in its place, nice big name tags on her luggage, I'll bet. On the other side of the slowly whirling steel contraption, he watched for the name. There it was. T. J. Carver. And there it was again. Brown and blue plaid luggage with wheels, maybe half a dozen pieces.

He sidled back the other way, this time watching the unsmiling woman in the black dress. She snatched at a square leather bag, scowled as she reached for another. The girl with the strange eyes captured two plaid suitcases, brown and blue. Joshua's heart leaped in his chest. "Oh, thank you, thank you, *thank you*, Grandfathers," he breathed.

"Thalia Carver?"

Tally jumped as two of her senses recorded him at her right. She didn't have to look. She knew immediately it was the bronze man she had erased from her memory banks just moments before. He smelled like something familiar: cedar smoke or turkey stuffing or Assateague's tall grasses. Oh, he smelled wonderful. She faced him.

"Sorry, ma'am." He twinkled at her from just the right distance above her face. "Didn't mean to scare you. Miz Carver, I'm Joshua Smith. Ezra Bangs The Drum sent me to get you. How many pieces of luggage?"

"How…how did you know it was me?" Tally stammered. She grabbed for a plaid travel case and missed it in her consternation. "Six!" She flushed angrily at his chuckle.

"Are they all those plaid ones, Miz Carver? Why don't you just sit down over there, and I'll collect them for you. Oh, I just figured it was you. They said you were real pale, with hair that blushed and eyes of several colors. I couldn't see another woman who fit that description. Although I was leaning toward that one over there at first."

His smile was sly as he gestured toward the harridan still battling her suitcases. Tally stifled a giggle as Joshua Smith busied himself with snagging each piece of her luggage.

The luggage cart raced ahead of her, and Tally fumed as she tried to keep up. She knew the sun turned her light brown hair into an apricot glow. Had someone really described her in that manner, for God's sake? Hair that blushed? Or was this…this Joshua Smith just full of himself? He was quiet now, content to let her follow along with him and the luggage. She broke the silence.

"Is it one o'clock here?" Tally had her waterproof Seiko in her hand, ready to change to Mountain Time.

"No watch, Miz Carver." Joshua Dale Smith squinted above, shading his eyes against the sun. "But I figure it's about one. Especially if that pretty little gold watch says it's three. You came from the East Coast, didn't you?"

Tally snapped the change of time into the watch and slid it back onto her faintly freckled wrist, just as he halted at a disreputable old Ford flatbed truck. Weathered picket fencing surrounded its wooden floor, and it overflowed with rolls of fencing and metal posts.

"I've got some tie-downs under the passenger seat, Miz Carver. Grab a few, and we'll secure this luggage back here, so it doesn't bounce around on the way to Poplar." He unhooked the rear gate on the picket fence and began to place the luggage carefully around the load of steel material. Tally Jo Carver had no idea what a tie-down was, but she opened the blue cab's door. J. D. SMITH, it read. NO JOB TOO SMALL.

A battered silver thermos lay in the middle of the bench seat, and there was a quarter-filled coffee cup in a beanbag cup holder on the floor. That smell! It was the scent of him, again. Tally's nostrils embraced the fragrance.

Ridiculous! You're ridiculous! she scolded herself, as she dug under the seat and came up with some bungee-like cords about two feet long with hooks at each end. The taste of his name was on her lips for the first time.

"These, Joshua?" She held up half a dozen tie-downs. "Are these enough?" She was slow to leave the scented cab, grateful she was not braless in a tee shirt, her usual travel garb.

He took them from her without a word, and made short work of attaching her luggage to the sides of the truck. She left the warm asphalt for the truck's interior, and he followed shortly. "It's over five hours to Poplar with this load on, Miz Carver—"

Tally interrupted him. "Please, call me Tally. Everyone does. I guess they'll call me Miz Carver in the Tribal office,

but my friends call me Tally. My mom calls me Tally Jo!
Okay?"

He nodded, taking in the new color in her eyes. It's the
blue of the upholstery, he thought. They're chameleon eyes.
My God, right now they're cold lake blue and a mile deep.
The tightening across his denim lap resisted his command
to subside.

"Okay, Tally. You will want to eat something before you
get to your new place. The store will be closed when we get
to Poplar, so you can't get groceries until tomorrow. What
would you like to eat?" The truck's floor shift responded
smoothly to the expert movements of his big, brown hands,
the load barely lurching as he rolled back, then forward to get
onto the airport exit road. He eyed her covertly, sideways, in
the rear-view mirror.

"Just a drive-through, if that's all right, Joshua. I really
want to get to the place before it gets dark. What's it like?
Have you been there?" Tally, usually self-possessed, heard
herself babbling.

"The apartment in Poplar, Tally, or the drive-through?"

He was laughing at her. Did he know how he affected
her? She sat quietly and let him continue.

"Yes, I've been in your apartment. I'm handyman to almost everybody in Poplar. It's a four-plex, about six years
old, built by the Valu-Wear Shoes folks to house their execu-
tives. Then they promoted tribal members to management,
and now only the General Manager lives there, so they rent
out the others. It's okay. Two bedrooms, but the furniture's
not much."

He pulled into Carl's Jr. and suggested she get a cup of
coffee for herself, so she'd have a cup to drink from on the

long ride to Poplar. He didn't suggest they sit at one of the tables to eat or argue when she insisted on paying the seven-dollar tab at the window. He understood perfectly her anxiety to get to her new home. As he spread two napkins across his lap and drove onto Highway 94 while munching on his Western Burger, she continued their conversation.

"My furniture's right behind me, Joshua. Part of the deal of my coming to Fort Peck. I had a one-bedroom place outside of Washington, so I'll probably have to get a few more pieces later. But Mr. Bangs The Drum said they would have 'the man' remove the furniture as soon as I asked." She took a bite of her burger and glanced sideways at him.

He was grinning. "Guess who 'the man' is, Tally?"

Was his voice low. seductive? Or was she imagining it?

"Oh. You?" Usually precise, she was befuddled again. "You're the delivery service and the take-away service and the pickup service and—" Tally stopped abruptly. She surely didn't want to sound like she was flirting with him. "And the fence-builder, too, I guess." She cast a glance at the load riding in reasonable quiet behind them.

He didn't answer, and she contented herself with the view from the truck's window. Tally was again astonished at the terrain. In grade school on Chincoteague, she had learned that Montana was a land of snow-capped mountains and deep green valleys. Now she knew that only described the western half of the state. This vista was why people called it the Big Sky Country. More like Big Round Sky, she thought. It was so flat. If you didn't look west, it was a round, level world, topped with a bowl of blue.

She saw a historical marker sign. "Oh, oh, I saw that when I drove this road and didn't have time to stop then, either.

The Little Big Horn Monument. Site of Custer's Last Stand. I sure hope to see it sometime."

There's hope for this white girl, Joshua Dale Smith considered. She didn't say "The Custer Massacre." He reached for his thermos and expertly poured half a cup of coffee. His nodded question at her coffee cup elicited a sweet, negative shake of her head. They traveled the next hundred miles of Big Sky Country in silence. Occasionally, he whistled, bits of an old tune she recognized: "The Girl from Ipanema."

The girl from Washington, D.C., this professional woman named Thalia Josephine Carver, was born on the mainland and raised on Chincoteague Island, off the Eastern Shore of Virginia. Her father, rarely in residence, was married to the Corps of Engineers. Their sprawling beach house was winterized and summerized, and Tally Jo's childhood was ideal.

There were other year-round children her age on Chincoteague. The island was a peninsula most of the year and had a stable population of about six thousand. In the summer, that number swelled to twenty thousand. Her mother rented out two rooms with breakfast every summer. Widowed these last two years, Tally's mom didn't need the money, but coveted the company.

Chincoteague's twin, Assateague, was about a quarter mile farther into the Atlantic. It was uninhabited, except for the ponies. Shetland ponies of all sizes and colors lived on Assateague. Its tall grasses sustained them, and Chincoteague's firemen visited with grain and salt if the usually mild winters grew harsh.

Once a year, the firemen held the Pony Fair. It was Chincoteague's big annual do. Firemen volunteers drove the bulk of the pony herd across the water and into makeshift pens on the Chincoteague beach. If you wanted a Misty of Chincoteague for your kid, you came to the auction at the Pony Fair. The firemen managed the money earned from the sale of the Shetlands, using it for the upkeep of Assateague and its ponies.

Tally had met Doug Holcomb at the University of Maryland. Her goal was an MBA, and she pursued all the accounting and business courses necessary. Douglas R. Holcomb pursued, among other young women, Tally Carver. A junior and pre-law, he intended to go to Yale Law School when he graduated. He saw her hair in the sunset one September evening, and followed her into the campus pizza parlor.

They were an item until they married, and they married because Tally was five weeks pregnant when she got her BA. He was finishing up at Maryland's Law School and had a job at prestigious Reston, Reston, Jones & Marshall in Washington waiting for him. She miscarried the week they moved into their Silver Spring apartment. He passed the bar on his second try and currently had a big job with a lobbyist firm and a big black book to keep track of his women.

She was loyal, couldn't understand infidelity, and divorced him for it. But loyalty and familiarity were her downfall. She allowed Doug to wander back to their apartment for an ocasional night or a weekend long after the divorce was final. He would drink too much, stroke her hair, and moan that she was the only woman for him.

Tally knew better. She would be twenty-eight in September and still couldn't break the ties that bound her to him, her first lover. At least, not until she saw the Fort Peck posting at the B.I.A., where she held a responsible Chief Accountant's position. *Controller needed for Eastern Montana*

Indian Reservation. She spoke to the head of her division of the Bureau of Indian Affairs, and here she was.

Here she was, indeed, on a highway that paralleled the Yellowstone River. "I'll be fueling up at Miles City, if you want to freshen up or anything." His voice fractured her reverie. Yes, she had only imagined it to be seductive. It was just a voice, masculine, and not well educated. She sat up straight and squared her shoulders.

"Thanks. I'll use the bathroom when you stop. Should I buy the fuel?"

He explained that he had intended to pick up the fencing in Billings today, anyway, and that Ezra would reimburse him for collecting Tally at the airport. She fumbled with the thermos and couldn't remove the vacuum cap. Joshua took it from her with his right hand. His large, callused hand covered hers for an instant. That instant made her squirm. Did he notice? No, she thought, he doesn't pay attention to anything but the road.

His years on the Seattle streets had made a silent watcher of Joshua Smith. He noticed, but made a rare misjudgment: this Tally Carver is uncomfortable with me. Probably hasn't been around Indians much, he told himself. Seems to be levelheaded, so she'll probably settle in. Grandfathers, she's a beauty.

Joshua guided the truck skillfully off the highway into a large truck stop. "Time to rest," he announced, and enjoyed the sight of her retreating form heading for the Mini-Mart and its rest rooms.

She was again perched stiffly inside the cab when he returned from his own ablutions. He eyed her profile as it wavered at him through the window glass. She had slicked her hair back into a ponytail now, tied with a bow of thick, black cord. The late afternoon sun bombarded her through the window, reflecting beams of the rose gold halo it made of the short hairs around her oval face. Joshua's breath quickened, and he pretended duty at the load of fencing for a minute.

Composure regained, he slung himself back into his driver's seat. Two brown sacks were at Tally's feet, and she was sipping from a 12-ounce cup of coffee. "I wasn't sure your thermos would last." She gestured with the coffee cup. "And I got some groceries for the house. Milk, juice, coffee, cheese, an apple. The five basic food groups."

He drove on, silent again for a while.

Tally, bored with the never-changing scenery, removed a thin sheaf of computer paper from her large, brown shoulder bag. She peered closely at the numbers and made tiny, legible marginal notes for eighty miles.

He asked her if she wanted to stop at Glendive. "I'm going to cut up to Wolf Point on the gravel. There's a rest stop on the High Line at Circle. It's about an hour. Or I'll stop here. Whatever."

She raised her head quickly and looked at him.

Those eyes are just kind of hazel, he scolded himself. Greenish-gray with brown spots. No big deal.

She shook her head to his question about stopping. "I guess I don't need to be working yet," she spoke professionally. "I have four days until Monday, when I'm officially the Controller of the Tribal Business Office. But Mr. Bangs The Drum sent me this financial statement when I accepted the job. And it seems like you don't want to talk while you drive." Relaxed again, leaning back against the upholstery, she continued to focus upon him.

Blue. Deep lake blue. Her eyes had switched again. Perhaps this woman was the trickster sent to lure him from sobriety's path. He'd go to the sweat lodge when he got home. "It's harder than it looks, keeping this load steady," he responded gruffly. Ashamed of the tone of his voice, Joshua sent her a soft smile to compensate. "Talk if you want to, Tally."

"Well, is there anything—any tips you could give me—about getting along? About being sure I am not offensive by accident? I just realized I don't know whether I should say 'Indian' or 'Native American,' for instance."

Now, he grinned, his white teeth brilliant against the full, bronze mouth. "I'll give you a tip, Tally. Don't count on controlling anything at that tribal office but the bookkeeping. You won't be controlling Chairman Bangs The Drum or the Tribal Council. Remember that, above all. And as for political correctness, I heard they're saying 'Amerind' now. For American Indian, I guess. We say Indian, but I guess Native American is best for you. Most of us don't pay any attention; we just look at the eyes."

It was a long speech, for him. She watched his serious face grow still again. He cast a glance across the cab at her rapt expression and quickly turned back to the road. *Under my skin, she is. And looking interested, just there. Hmmm.*

On the other side of Circle at Highway 200, which Joshua called the High Line, they stopped at a primitive rest area.

"Coffee runs through me, Tally. I have to 'rest' here."

She left the cab for the weed-choked gravel as her companion disappeared into a rustic chemical toilet and was stepping in place the fiftieth time when he emerged.

Joshua's heart soared. The glorious girl, hair shining in the western sun, grabbed at his senses as no woman ever had.

He started to speak and had to clear his choked-up throat. "Ahem...er...Tally." Joshua struggled for words. "Would you like to take a side trip? There are some amazing buffalo wallows about ten miles over." Would you like to camp out on the prairie with me, roll in my blanket, only the stars to see? His brain wrote lyrics to the soul music his heart sang at the sight of her.

She glanced at her watch, loathe to break the connection between them, but torn by her devotion to making and working a plan. "We can still get to Poplar long before dark, can't we?" Tally asked.

The moment was gone. Joshua strolled deliberately to his side of the truck, got in and started the engine. "C'mon, Miz Carver," he intoned politely. "We're burnin' daylight."

Nearly an hour to Wolf Point, and the only sound was gravel crunching under the truck's heavy tires. An occasional rock tumbled into a metal wheel well, its clatter shattering the silence. Tally was dumbstruck. What could she say to rekindle the interest she was sure he had shown in her? Should she have gone with him on the side trip? What was a buffalo wallow? She slumped and sighed.

"Here's the Missouri, Tally. After we cross over on the new bridge here, we'll be on the reservation and in Wolf Point. You've heard of the Wolf Point Stampede?"

She hadn't.

"Well, Poplar is just twenty-two miles east. You're nearly home. Another safe trip, I reckon." He was turning onto a paved highway as he spoke, and smiling at her in the mirror. Tally seized the moment.

"Joshua. Joshua, I appreciate the safe trip, and I would really have liked to see the buffalo wallows. Maybe you'd take me to them another time?" She leaned toward him a little and patted his shoulder. The palm of her hand tingled at the brief contact, and she withdrew it as casually as possible.

"More coffee, please." He teased her as he deftly opened the thermos with one hand and gave it to her for pouring. "We can drink it up now, since we're on the home stretch. I'd like to show you the buffalo wallows, Tally, and Fort Peck Dam and Square Butte and—" Joshua dropped his voice and concentrated on the road for a minute. When he resumed conversation, his voice was friendly, impersonal.

"After you get settled in, Tally Jo Carver. After you're un- packed, I'll take you exploring. Okay?" They sipped coffee in comfortable silence until the stark reservation town loomed ahead on the highway. On the outskirts of Poplar, he drove a short way on a macadam street and parked in front of Tally's new home.

It was nicely maintained. Two apartments were upstairs, two down, and the redwood stain on the trim and stairs was recent. Chain link fencing enclosed about half an acre of newly mown grass. "You have a covered parking spot in the rear," Joshua said, gesturing toward the back of the property.

Tally's hand was on the door handle. She didn't want to leave the sight and sound of him, the scent of this cab. He got out and came around, opening her door from the outside.

"Madame," Joshua flourished. "I have your keys, courtesy of Ezra Bangs The Drum, and would be proud to escort you and your ton of luggage upstairs." He offered his bronzed arm, half-wrapped in its pale denim sleeve. She put her arm on his shoulder theatrically and prepared to float down from the Ford.

A dominant male voice disintegrated the moment. The man was hurrying across the green of the lawn from a lower apartment. He was over six feet tall, slender, with neat brown hair, silvered at the temples. Even his pressed Dockers were imposing. He spoke with authority. "Thalia Carver?"

Chapter Two

The split second Tally's hand rested on Joshua's muscled forearm was electric, and she jerked it away. "Yes, that's me," she answered the intruder, as she stepped onto the macadam and faced the good-looking man approaching through the gate. "And here I am!"

"I'm Gerry Marsden, General Manager of the Valu-Wear Shoes factory here on the Fort Peck reservation, Ms. Carver." His handshake was firm, his hand smooth. "We're your landlords, and I've made your apartment as ready as can be. Lights, telephone tomorrow, those kinds of things. The last tenants left in a hurry, so we also had it professionally cleaned for you." Marsden situated himself between Joshua and Tally. "Shall we get your bags upstairs?"

The men let Tally carry a small case and her paper sacks of provisions, and the trio got the luggage upstairs in one trip. Joshua placed the plaid suitcases carefully next to the worn welcome mat in front of 2-B, and prepared to open the door with the key ring he'd extracted from his breast pocket. Gerry Marsden took the keys from him with a friendly smile.

"I'll take it from here, Smith. Thanks for your help. Oh, that back patch still has to be cleared of debris. Can you get to it this month?" Marsden was through the door, dismissing Joshua. When he turned to hold the door for Tally, he was dismayed to find she was walking slowly to the stairs with the Indian.

Gerry reached for a bag and used it to prop open the door. He began to place suitcases noisily, one at a time, just inside the apartment door. Tally was oblivious, lingering at the top of the stairs, talking with Joshua in a lowered voice.

"Thanks so much, Joshua. Really. I did enjoy the ride here. I guess I'll see you when you take the furniture out, probably Friday?" She took his right hand as if for a handshake. It became a mutual caress.

Gerald Marsden leaned on the doorjamb and watched with disdain as Joshua Smith's right palm left her hand and patted the girl's face with an indescribable tenderness. He didn't hear Joshua's soft words. "Oh, yes. You'll see me, Tally. 'Bye, now."

After he left, Joshua's watchful eyes noted the lights going on inside apartment 2-B. He surveyed the outside surroundings, softened by the oncoming dusk. Weed fields lay beyond the chain link fence surrounding the apartment building. The mini-storage was between here and the highway, vacant lots from here until Main Street. Except for the apartment building itself, Tally didn't have neighbors.

A white couple and a Sioux mother with a child lived in two of the apartments, Marsden himself in the third. The single mother worked at the shoe factory. He didn't know anything about the couple yet, and Joshua was concerned. 2-B's former tenants had left Poplar a step ahead of State, City, and Tribal Law just a month ago. They'd been distributing eight balls and some crack cocaine from that apartment, and he was certain the lock had not been changed.

Be safe, Tally Jo Carver, Joshua intoned to himself as he started up the Ford. He headed into Poplar to take his kids to supper, hoping all the way that their grandmother, Jo Ellen Warbonnet Red Leggins, would not be on the warpath tonight. His thoughts drifted back to sixteen years ago, before the children were born.

He'd married Jilly Red Leggins when he had finished just one quarter of the college year at Montana State in Bozeman. She was seventeen, a senior at Poplar High School, and pregnant with James-Dale. He and Jilly had been sweethearts since grade school and drinking buddies since he was fifteen, and they had always intended to get married some day. If Joshua had been able to stay in college, he would have been overjoyed at marriage and fatherhood.

As it was, he acclimated well enough to the workaday world of a hard-drinking family man. He worked as a ranch hand for his grandfather, Raymond Wooden Headdress. When Ellen Joy was born the next year, he and Jilly and the children left Jo Ellen's house and rented Tribal housing. They drank and fought and made up and loved their brown babies, cherished their chubby toddlers.

Jilly liked to party in Wolf Point or Scobey with others from their old high school crowd. Jo Ellen and Jilly's little sister, Christy, were glad to babysit with James-Dale and the baby girl while Joshua was working. Thus it was that Jilly and three of her friends died in the head-on collision outside Wolf Point that summer thirteen years ago.

Joshua was a widower at twenty-one, with a mother-in-law who somehow blamed him for his wife's death. Before the year was out, he had left the children with Jo Ellen and twelve-year-old Christy, so he could escape the reservation and "get his head on straight."

Yeah, really straight, Joshua told himself, as he pulled into the driveway of Jo Ellen's neat Poplar home. Nine years, basically all of them spent drunk on the streets of Seattle. Back home and sober these three years now, he could see Jo Ellen was warming up, beginning to trust him. Give her time, he thought. Give them all time. He knocked on the screen door at Jo Ellen's porch, stood for a moment, and then stepped into the front room.

It was full of the organized clutter of the grandmother's occupation. Assiniboine Star Quilts, sold on consignment to the local trading post and the one at Wolf Point, earned Jo Ellen a fine living. Seated in her easy chair, she was stitching a quilt top. A Jerry Springer melodrama oozed from the 25-inch television.

"Hi, Joshua." She greeted him without smiling and drew her coarse, still black hair away from her eyes with a dark brown hand. "Kids are in the back." Her bulky body turned again to the television show. She hadn't missed a stitch.

"O-ho, Miss Christmas!" Joshua greeted his children's aunt, who was washing dishes at the stainless double sink in the big, square kitchen. Christmas Joy Red Leggins was now twenty-five, still single and living at home with her mother. She had worked her way up to a responsible position at the shoe factory, starting there right out of high school. The beautiful half-Sioux, half-Assiniboine girl was her mother's only living child. A car had struck and killed Jo Ellen's middle child, Matthew, on the highway five years after Jilly's death. Her husband and two of her three children had been lost to booze, and Jo Ellen Warbonnet Red Leggins was an outspoken teetotaler.

"O-ho to you, Joshua Dale Smith." Christy lifted her almond eyes from the dishwater to smile at her brother-in-law. "They're out back with the new puppy. Hey, howcum you never take me out to eat, only the brat kids? Huh?" She giggled nervously to cover the enormity of her question. Christy's crush on thirty-four-year-old Joshua was not yet apparent to him.

"Want to come, Christy? You're more than welcome. We're going to the rib joint in Wolf Point. I promised, if James-Dale would bring his algebra up to C or better on his last report card. I just know it'll be ribs once a week all summer! But worth it. A kid can't get far without math these days." Joshua was heading for the open back door; excited puppy yelps filtered through the screen. When he was sure Christy wasn't going to answer him, he stood at the door.

"The bus for Ribsville is leaving, my children! All aboard or stay thee home!" Two pretty teenagers with shoulder-length hair looked up from a fat, yellow puppy.

"Hey, dad," Ellen Joy said. "Boy, am I starvin'! Grandma wouldn't let us have anything, so we wouldn't spoil our supper. C'mon, James-Dale, let's move it!"

"Better not let your Great-Grandpa Raymond see that little beauty there, James-Dale," Joshua teased his son. "That guy is just right for puppy-tail soup!" He wasn't sure his aged Grandfather's stories of special soup at the Red Bottom Days of a bygone era were true, but he loved to listen to Raymond Wooden Headdress's stories, treasured since he was a tiny boy.

Ellen was fourteen and had just finished her freshman year at Poplar High School, an honor student. Already as tall as her father by virtue of her Sioux heritage, she was leading scorer on the junior varsity basketball team and 'sixth man' on the varsity squad. The Poplar girls had gone to State this spring, and expected to go and win it all next year. She came easily to hug her dad.

James-Dale, at fifteen, was the spitting image of his sister, and just the same height. Both children had Jilly's smooth, oval face and eyes. A sophomore, his grades were mediocre and his interests seemed to be in debate and drama. He had received rave reviews in a minor role in the Poplar High School's annual Spring Play, and hoped to win the lead role next year.

James-Dale worked spring to fall with his own riding mower and gas edger, maintaining the lawns of the well-to-do and the retired of Poplar. Joshua suspected his son had been having a occasional beer this summer, and watched for an opening to talk with him.

The boy deposited the puppy in a blanket-stuffed doghouse and came into the house. "How, dad," he greeted his father, raising his hand with the palm outward and standing a body distance away. Joshua didn't think it was funny, but smiled, anyway.

Christy had changed to a bright shirt over her jeans, brushed her hair and glossed her lips. She tried to appear nonchalant as she joined the threesome. "You've got the truck, Joshua; we'll have to take my car." Joshua was pleasantly surprised that Christy was joining them. Jo Ellen glowered as they exited the front door.

"No drinking, Christmas Joy Red Leggins! Joshua Smith, not one beer in that dear girl, do you hear me!" Jo Ellen yelled. She stitched and watched the television screen while the two adults and two teenagers piled into Christy's six-year-old Toyota, but her countenance softened as she continued her work, alone in the house. Joshua was a fine father, no drink for several years now, supported the children proudly, and Christy was interested in him. Jo Ellen stitched and thought and stitched some more.

"I just love to be chauffeured, Miss Christmas!" Joshua teased Christy the same way he had ever since she was Jilly's ten-year-old sister. "Are you for hire?"

She flashed him a scornful look from the driver's seat. She was as beautiful as Jilly had been, but did not look like her, except in times like this. When angry, she looked and sounded like his dead wife.

"Would you have offered to drive if I were some other woman, Joshua?"

He heard the tremor in her voice and knew he was on dangerous ground right now. What was going on with the pretty, young sister-in-law these days? He tried to placate her. "C'mon, Christy. It's a rib party. And I've never known a woman yet who would let me drive her car!"

She made a face at him and the foursome chattered comfortably all the way to Wolf Point.

In her new apartment, Tally was refusing Gerald Marsden's offer of more help that evening. "Call me Tally, won't you? Thalia was a great-aunt with lots of money who didn't leave me any, anyway!" She laughed as she explained her old-fashioned name. "And I'll call you Gerry or Gerald or whatever you prefer."

A rummage through the biggest, heaviest plaid bag produced the pieces of a 4-cup coffeepot, a can opener, and four stacked, plastic cups. Her attention to detail was evident in the neatly packed bag. Every possible bit of space was in use. She took some coffee filters from the cups as she spoke.

"Will you have coffee with me before you go?" Tally hinted politely at the handsome man sprawled in a well-worn orange recliner. "If you don't take sugar, that is. I do have milk." She assembled the pot expertly and had coffee brewing within a minute.

From the overflowing bag, Tally removed a set of striped sheets and a fringed afghan. She went to the hallway and looked again at the bedrooms. The one across from the bathroom was the larger, so she tossed the bedding onto that double bed. "Be glad when my furniture comes," she called back to Gerry. "Don't much care for the Early Salvation Army bedroom furniture in here!"

His raucous laughter was loud at her shoulder, and she jumped. He was right behind her.

"Oh, sorry, Tally," he apologized in his polite voice, patting her shoulder in a non-threatening manner. "I was just making sure they cleaned everything well. I checked the refrigerator; it's cold and clean." Tally squeezed by him and went back to the kitchen. There she put her milk, juice, cheese, and apple into the white cavern of the refrigerator.

Her mother had taught Tally well. Southern hospitality conversation in her melodic voice brightened the bleak apartment. "How long have you been here on Ft. Peck, Gerry? Is there anything I should know before I go to work Monday? Do you think Mr. Bangs The Drum will be over to see me before then?" Only a fetching trace of Virginia idiom coated her speech.

"Six years now, Tally." Marsden's long body stretched out in the armchair again. He poked his nose in the air and sniffed with a beatific smile, a gesture of appreciation for the coffee aroma beginning to permeate the room. "I'm originally from Sioux Falls, South Dakota. They offered me this new factory right after my divorce, and it sounded like a good idea. Fresh start and all. The home office is in Connecticut, and I think they thought any native of Sioux Falls, South Dakota knew all about Indians. I don't think I'd seen a dozen of them altogether until I got here!" He snickered at the little joke on his superiors and rose to take his coffee from her.

A free hand patted her arm as he took the cup, and she looked into his deep-set gray eyes. The return gaze was sensual, and she was certain he was going to kiss her. She wondered if she was interested even as she retreated backwards, careful not to give offense. No sense spilling hot coffee on a nice-looking, obviously interested fellow, she thought. Kisses can wait for another day. Like—tomorrow?

Two good-looking guys in one day, Miss Tally? Wonder what's on the agenda for Thursday? This Montana isn't at all bad, is it? She giggled at her silly thoughts as she placed her cup on the shiny blond coffee table and slumped to the couch. "Sorry, Gerry. Nothing you said. I'm just a little rummy from jet lag, I think." She looked at her watch. "It's after ten in Washington, and I'm an early-to-bed girl."

He had waited for her to ask questions about his divorce, family, and other usual first-conversation chatter. Tally wasn't the usual young woman. She didn't ask personal questions, and he didn't see any future in pushing the relationship any further at this time.

Marsden made a little tableau of hurrying to finish his coffee and rose to his feet. "No, no, don't get up, Tally! I'll look in on you tomorrow at noon. If it's okay with you, I'll take you to lunch. Now, I'm right below you, so don't worry about a thing." He crossed the desert colors of the kitchen tile and, with a little wave, let himself smoothly out the door.

Weary, Tally sagged back against the worn brown cushion. As her eyes closed, she thought of Joshua. She saw his black eyes, full mouth and the bulges of his body. She imagined the scent of his shirt. The sweet, grassy odor was still in her nostrils as she hugged herself and fell into exhausted sleep.

She awakened reluctantly, shivering, groping for blankets that were not there. The apartment was cold and damp, rather musty, and her limbs were stiff from sleeping in an upright position. It was 2:10 on the little watch on her wrist; just enough light issued from the kitchen to read the dial.

A noisy car passed close by, and she heard a yell—two yells?—in the distance, and was frightened for a split second. Usually levelheaded, she shrugged it off and rose quickly to check the main door in the kitchen. Gerry Marsden had left it unlocked.

Tally threw the key-locked deadbolt and set the lock on the knob. Now she was curious about the French doors that led to the small deck off the living room and retrieved a small, powerful torch from the biggest suitcase on the kitchen floor. Thus armed, she switched it on and crossed the living room to open the double doors.

The wooden deck was about 5 x 8 feet. The bright beam from the flashlight illuminated a rusting barbecue pan on a tiny, faded redwood table. A black metal ladder hung on the narrow inside wall to her left. It was icy in the chill June night. Her light picked up large metal grommet holes in the floor of the deck on her left, the railing purposely built to accommodate the ladder. "My fire escape," she chortled softly. Remembering she had close neighbors, she put her finger to her lips. Shh, Tally. Oh, but this is great. It takes a cat burglar to get in the back way!

Tally gazed westward as she backed into her living room and saw the moving lights of a lone car on the highway just a few blocks away. An unbroken view of the horizon in the starlight captivated her. You're a long way from our nation's capital, Tally girl! She tested that both locks on the knobs were set, and vowed to leave them that way always. Taking one more look into the starry Montana night, she drew the heavy drape over the French doors.

The bathroom was glistening clean, and Tally thanked her lucky stars. Chrome and plastic shower doors enclosed an enamel tub, banged up but scoured and dry. Oak cabinets lined the south wall under the sink, with a large oak medicine chest and three-way mirror countersunk into the wall above. She washed her hands and face and left the light burning to guide her to the bedroom.

Both pillowcases went on one striped pillow and she smoothed a sheet onto the bare, new mattress. Back in the kitchen, Tally poured a cup of milk and ate a finger of string cheese. A fluffy housecoat came from one of the smaller plaid bags, and she extinguished lights as she returned to her bedroom.

The room was about twelve feet square. Windows on both the south and west walls were shuttered with narrow, impersonal venetian blinds. She used the attached plastic rod on each to turn the closed slats up for less visibility from the outside. That done, she hung her lonely jacket on one of several empty hangers in the large closet, and stepped out of her khaki pants, white shirt, and beige bra and panties. Too cold in here, she thought as she stretched. I'll figure out the heat before I shower in the morning.

There was a nice full-length mirror on the inside of the bedroom door, and she pushed the door closed to look at her unclothed body. Her tousled, thick, shoulder-length hair looked pale brown in the yellow bedroom light. Her skin was smooth and fair, even with the remains of last year's tan. High, heavy breasts tipped with deep rose overlooked a small waist, round hips, long legs. Tally hid the end of her thumb in her navel, and grinned as she pirouetted to observe her profile. Only a puff of apricot fuzz showed below her belly.

Wrapped in the blue robe, she shut off the light. The unfamiliar bed was uncomfortable only for the moment it took her to snuggle into her old, mother-knitted afghan. Tally Jo Carver slept again, peaceful in her new Montana home.

A silent watcher sat on the empty side road a block away. His view of both Tally's rear deck and front walkway was unobstructed. A six-pack of cans was in a red plastic cooler beside him, two empties on the floor. A lumpy plastic sack, obtained in Wolf Point before dark, sat next to the cooler. It sang a metallic tune when his hand brushed its contents, reaching again and again into the cooler.

He had been there since full dark, about ten o'clock. He was certain she was alone, for just as the Poplar Bar and Grill closed she had awakened. He saw her come onto her deck with a small, bright light. In silhouette with pale light behind her, she had stood at her doorway and looked into the night. His heart raced at the sight of her.

Later, it was as if she signaled to him with the click-click of the lights behind her bedroom blinds. He knew she was in her bedroom when that light went off and no others glowed. He imagined her undressing, peeling off her underthings and smoothing a nightgown over that wonderful body. He was aroused and sat still as a statue, watching.

Chapter Three

The eastern sky was only threatening to pale when Tally's apartment lit up like a Christmas tree. His long night's vigil was over. Several forlorn aluminum cans that had once brimmed with lemon tea littered the truck's floorboard. The nearly empty thermos on the seat beside him seemed similarly abandoned.

His capable hand reached into the plastic sack and patted the metal objects. Good, strong, key-lock dead bolt and handset here, he congratulated himself. I won't have to worry tomorrow night. Or watch.

Joshua Smith checked the streets right and left to be sure nothing bigger than a raccoon was moving, then started his engine. She's unpacking, he thought. I'll go on out home and get cleaned up, get back to her place after I set these fence posts for John Big Elk.

To the dark morning, he breathed a prayer. Oh, Grandfathers. Grandfathers, is this white girl really to be my love?

Tally awakened with a start, and it took a minute to get her bearings. I'm in my apartment in Poplar, Montana, she said to herself before she opened her eyes. I'm under Mama's afghan, and my own furniture will be here tomorrow. I am going to love this place.

Thus encouraged, she opened her eyes to the bare white walls of her new bedroom. She found a shiny electric wall heater in the bathroom and punched the ON button. In her comfortable kitchen, Tally switched on the light and wondered at the absence of sunlight in the eastern window. A glance at her watch told her the reason. Her body was still on Eastern Daylight Time. It was 4:45 AM here in Montana.

"Oh, well," she said to her French doors as she opened the drapes, "I'll get an early start. Wonder what time the grocery store opens. Wonder where it is!" She started a four-cup pot of coffee and began unloading the big, open case on the kitchen floor. A small saucepan and skillet were among the items she took from it. She poured a cup of coffee, took two towels, a washcloth, and her overnight case, and headed for the warming bathroom.

Joshua's flatbed traveled slowly toward the highway. He turned his head to see if he could catch a glimpse of her on the deck again. Better watch yourself, he admonished. Don't go biting off something you can't chew. He did not see Tally and, splashing in the shower, she did not hear his heavily laden truck creep toward home.

He thought about last night's supper as he drove the six roundabout miles to the small trailer he called home. It was obvious that Christy was interested in him as more than a brother-in-law, and all he could do was wonder how long he had been oblivious to her interest. She had hugged him goodnight without a sisterly bone in her sweet-smelling body. I'll have a good talk with her without hurting her feelings, he promised himself, as he pulled into the private road he'd built by hand.

The pretty forty acres by the river was part of his dead mother's land allotment, which he'd inherited on her death when he was fourteen. This, and a hundred sixty acres that was part of Raymond Headdress's ranch, was trust land. He owned it, but the B.I.A. controlled it, as it controlled Rosie's two hundred acres of the Headdress grazing land.

Ten years of lease money was on his books when he came back to Fort Peck, and he had been grateful the Agency was unable to find him in Spokane. He had improved this parcel with the accumulated $3300, and hauled the trailer from the ranch with his grandfather's blessing.

Engineer came soundlessly from his hideout under the trailer. His black and tan muzzle leaned excitedly against his master's hip. Mazurka nickered from the sturdy lean-to at the sound of the truck. She was asking about last night's grain. Joshua and the German shepherd went to give her the overdue evening treat.

"Hey, girl. Did you miss me?" She nuzzled at his chest with her blazed chestnut nose as he placed the oats mixture in front of her. "Hey! Hey, watch it," he chided her, as she pulled at the snaps on his shirt. Joshua laid his face against the filly's nose for a moment.

"I met a woman, my friends. My God, what a woman! I am probably in love this morning!" Mazurka snorted and chewed at her grain, while Engineer danced deftly around Joshua's legs. "She's a white girl. Real smart, too, I think. But..." Joshua preened and flexed his biceps, alone and silly with his four-legged confidantes "...I think she likes me, anyway!"

He perked coffee while he took a quick shower and donned a clean denim work shirt. He brushed his lengthening black hair back and secured it with a rawhide string. A stubby ponytail reflected in the mirror. Three years uncut, his hair barely reached his shoulders. Finally, he snapped, and then unsnapped, the top closure of his shirt while looking at himself in the bathroom mirror. "Ah, the hell with it!" He grimaced at his rare curse, snapped the shirt for the last time, and went to fill his thermos. It was nearly full daylight, and he could start setting the posts.

Mazurka nickered again. "No, I haven't forgotten you, good girl." Joshua rattled the halter needlessly, for she was already on her way to the gate. He took her near the river to lush grass, staked her out on a long rope, and hugged her again.

"Stay, Engineer," he commanded the dog. "Stay!" The fierce, territorial guardian would see that no harm befell Mazurka or the property. He pointed the truck back to Red Elk's ranch, north of Poplar.

It was 8:30 AM. Tally picked up the phone for the sixth time since eight o'clock. The instrument had no dial tone. "Oh, well. They always say between eight and noon," she said to the French doors. "But I do want to call Mayflower and see when my van will be here. And I should call Mr. Bangs The Drum, too." She opened the doors to create a cross draft and stepped into the brilliant sunshine on her tiny deck.

"I'll have to get a small patio chair," she continued, talking out loud just to hear a voice. "No, make that two of them, just in case!" Laughing, she thought of the two different men, Joshua and Gerry. "Maybe I'll get three. That sounds rather interesting!" Tally went back to her bedroom and took a nap.

Rrrnnng. Rrnng. She awakened with a start, groping first for the phone, and then for an alarm clock. She hurried, groggy, to the living room to answer the phone.

"Hello? Hello?" *Now* there was a dial tone. She replaced the beige receiver and turned away in disgust. It rang again.

"Hello, Tally. This is Gerry Marsden." Tally looked at her watch as he talked. She had slept another three hours. "I'd like to come by around 12:30 and take you to lunch. Does that work for you?"

Half an hour to get presentable would work just fine. "I'll be ready, Gerry. Thanks."

She walked through the shower, and put on her new Montana clothes. After a moment's hesitation at the bathroom counter, she added a dab of her killer perfume.

She stood at the top of the stairs waiting for him. Ordinarily unflappable, Marsden stood a moment with his hand on the chain link gate. What a sight she is, he thought, even in those tourist clothes. Just look at that hair!

Tally was a picture to grace the cover of *Western Women* magazine. Her tan, pearl-buttoned shirt wasn't new, but she'd purchased the calf-length, divided skirt and knee boots of whipcord brown especially for leisure in Montana. Her soft leather belt matched the high-heeled boots, and a blue and brown scarf placed its knot at the pulse in her throat.

He stood at the bottom of the covered stairway and held out his hand. "Gosh, you're gorgeous today, ma'am." Gerry was acting as western as her outfit. "What, no ten-gallon hat? We must buy you one at the local haberdashery."

"Oh, Gerry." She was now concerned. "Is this too much? I was so taken with it in the store, and it looked like Montana to me. But no, I don't think I'm the cowboy hat type. Too short."

She reached the bottom riser, and Gerry took both her hands. He looked into her uncommon, spotted green eyes. "I hope to never hear you say that again, Miz Carver. If anyone ever was just the right height, or dressed exactly perfectly, it is you."

Neither of them noticed the Ford flatbed, which passed silently, now empty of its fencing, and did not slow down. Joshua's heart seized as he tried to interpret the scene in front of Tally's apartment building. Okay, Grandfathers, he thought, it's okay. I'll just leave it up to you. He turned back toward town, to do the porch repair at Jackie Moses'. He'd return to Tally's after Marsden went back to the factory.

Lunch was at a little café in the heart of Poplar. "Owned and operated by locals," Gerry explained to her. "I like to patronize them. And the food isn't bad."

There were about twenty customers eating lunch there, brown faces and white. Their waitress was a round, happy woman with a big button on her denim shirt. It said, "I'm Blue Cloud. I'm Sioux." She called Gerry "Mr. Marsden," and was deferential as she gave them water and menus. Gerry did not introduce the waitress to her.

"What's the special, Norma Jean?" Gerry asked the waitress.

She smiled and shrugged her shoulders in resigned acceptance. "Indian taco and salad, sir. Four dollars, fifty cents. It's very good today."

Gerry looked across the scarred booth at Tally. "It's a taco mixture on Indian fry bread. Really good, if you like tacos." When Tally nodded, he spoke again to the waitress.

"Two specials. Two coffees. Thanks." Effectively dismissing her with a turn of his body, he focused his attention on Tally.

"Apartment to your liking?" he asked. "I'm glad the phone is working for you already. Do you know when your stuff will be here?"

"It will be fine, Gerry. Tell me, why does Norma Jean's badge say her name is Blue Cloud?" Tally's eyes had not left the departing waitress.

"Oh, I think she just does it for fun. For tourists, you know. Her husband works for me. Her name is Norma Jean Ransome on all his paperwork. We employ 212 at the factory, Tally, most of them tribal members, although Ransome isn't. We have medical and dental for them, and pay pretty well, besides. We have greatly increased the standard of living on the Fort Peck reservation in the last six years."

Gerry fluttered his hands and gave a self-deprecating grin. "I talk too much. My work, you know. About all I'm involved in. Tell me, Tally, about you. Where did you go to school?"

They were still chatting, new acquaintance conversation, when their giant lunch specials came. He had three teenaged children in Connecticut, she learned, and flew there each summer on his vacation.

"Indian taco, singular?" Tally hissed with pleasure. "I think mine is at least a three-Indian taco!" Nonetheless, she demolished it with obvious enjoyment and little conversation.

"I love a woman who eats with gusto," Marsden observed. "Although, I must say," and here he took in her body in its new outfit, "I don't know where you put it."

"I suppose you have to get back, Gerry," she replied, ignoring his interest in her body. "And I have to call Mayflower and the agent to get my rental insurance transferred, and call Mr. Bangs The Drum, and get the furniture taken out—"

"The furniture's all arranged, Tally. That fellow Smith who picked you up at the airport? He'll take it away, but feel free to keep anything in there you may need." Gerry was signaling for the check.

"Was everything okay?" Their sunny waitress asked the usual question.

Tally began to answer. "Oh, it was—"

Marsden interrupted her again. "Just fine, Norma Jean."

Did he sound pompous as he handed over his credit card? Tally was uncertain, but not willing to let him dismiss the woman so abruptly.

"Blue Cloud." Tally's voice caused the woman to turn in their direction. "Thanks for suggesting the Indian taco. It is my first Montana meal, and I'll always remember it."

As he opened the car door, Gerry's hand patted the side of her neck when she stooped to enter. A caress. That's definitely a caress, she thought. "Home, James!" Tally Carver joked when she was confused.

"I just hope you'll always remember who you shared your first Montana meal with, too, Miss Tally." Gerry watched the road as he spoke. "I also hope we can do some other things together when you get settled."

"I'd like that, Gerry," Tally promised. His perfect profile was pleased as he drove, expertly and in silence.

She insisted that he drop her off, since they'd been gone much more than a lunch hour. It impressed her that he sat on the street until she had let herself into the apartment. A blast of the apartment's stale odor assailed her nostrils when she unlocked the door. She locked the screen door and left it open, then cracked the French doors to again create a cross draft.

From the deck, she spotted Joshua Smith's truck. It was turning the corner from the side street down there. Tally sensed that it stopped at her apartment building as she raced to smooth her hair and dust powder on her nose. She greeted him at the kitchen door with feigned nonchalance.

"Tally Jo Carver. Nice skirt. Do you ride?"

"Er, ah, well…yes. A little. Well…no, not really. Ponies, mostly, at home. I guess this is a riding skirt, isn't it?"

Joshua was removing pliers, a screwdriver, and a plastic-wrapped lockset from the paper bag he carried. His wink was conspiratorial. "Good idea you had, Miz Carver, changing this lock. It was not changed when the unsavory former tenants left town. I'll just put the charges on my next bill to Valu-Wear. Is this what you had in mind?" He handed her the plastic hardware store package. It was identical to the existing knob on the kitchen door.

"I'm just full of good ideas today, Joshua Smith," Tally bantered as he went to work with the screwdriver. "For instance, why don't you take the furniture out today, if you have time? Leave the small bed and dresser and one—no, make it two—of these kitchen chairs. I'll rough it until my furniture comes, and then the Mayflower men can just put everything in the right place." Pleased with herself, she took a breath.

"Why two?" He didn't waste words, she noticed.

Tally was speechless. Why two, indeed? "Uh…in case I want to sit on the deck. And one just looks…lonely."

"Mm hm," he assented, as he removed the old doorknob and replaced it with the new one he'd brought. He was whistling "The Girl From Ipanema."

"Well, can you, Joshua? Take the furniture out today?"

"Can and will, Tally. Then, after your moving van gets here, I'll pick up the two chairs. Before they get a chance to get lonely."

Was he teasing her? He wasn't smiling. Tally's composure was shaken again. She wanted to get closer to him, to see if he smelled like yesterday. "Cup of coffee, Joshua?"

"Thought you'd never ask, Tally. I had my hands full and didn't bring my thermos up." She poured a plastic cup of this morning's coffee and advanced the four steps to take it to him.

Joshua laid his tools on the kitchen table, removed two brass screws from his mouth, and laid them carefully beside the pliers. He surrounded her hand with his two large ones. "Thank you for giving me to drink in your home."

The strange words and his courtly manner touched her. A chill ran up the back of her neck into her scalp. She was rooted to the spot when he spoke again.

"Not bad. I'm a connoisseur of fine coffee. You do right well with that dinky little coffeepot."

She beamed at his almost-praise and thought, Today he smells kind of horsy, too. She sat at one of the chairs she would place on the deck later, and gloried in watching him work.

CHAPTER FOUR

Gerry Marsden ran upstairs at least half a dozen times over the weekend. He offered a broom and dustpan, a radio, a trip to Wolf Point or Glasgow for dinner. He eyed the coffee hungrily on most of his visits.

Tally was flattered at his persistence, but anxious to make her new home "just so" before she went to work Monday morning. She wasn't sure she would even stop for coffee with Joshua, should that taciturn gentleman happen to come by.

He didn't come by. She hadn't seen him since he removed the furniture. On his last trip up the stairs, he asked her if he might smudge the entry with its new lock. She was silently overjoyed that she knew about "smudge" from contemporary Indian reading, and she agreed it would be a good thing.

It was the sweet grass he burned that smelled so wonderful. The odor hung around him and in his truck, she realized, as he made his brief ceremony and left her. The faintness of it now lingered. She wandered to the kitchen end of the apartment each night before she went to bed, inhaling deeply and wondering about the silent man, Joshua Dale Smith.

"Ask me about something for next weekend, Gerry," she told the Valu-Wear general manager, when he asked her to go out. "About mid-week, when I find out how tired I am from the new job." He said he'd hold her to it.

Her compact, last-model Olds Cutlass had ridden well behind the Mayflower van, and it was good to have wheels again. She used it on Friday afternoon to go to the local grocery. On Sunday, with most of her boxes unpacked and the computer up and running in the little bedroom, Tally treated herself to a drive around Poplar. She circumnavigated, and then criss-crossed the town, making sure she knew the route to work for Monday morning.

Montana people waved when you met their cars on the road, she noticed. It was fun to wave at them first, although she was quick to note that pedestrians did not greet strangers in automobiles, nor did they return her wave. It was flat, brown, and unlovely here in Poplar, and she hoped Joshua would take her to see the beautiful sights soon.

Monday morning, she introduced herself to the woman at the reception desk. "I'm Tally Carver, the Tribe's new controller. Mr. Bangs The Drum expects me today."

"He's not in yet," said the young woman, not reciprocating Tally's introduction.

Tally ignored the receptionist's apathetic attitude. "Would you point me to the accounting office, please?" She followed the pointed finger up a wide stairway to a huge, messy office. Half a dozen clerks were having coffee and donuts to start their day.

"Hi, there!" Tally smiled and put her briefcase on a vacant chair. "I'm your new controller. I'd just like to go to my office until Mr. Bangs The Drum gets in. We'll do introductions later." Two of the younger Indian women leaped up and herded Tally to the hallway behind the outer office, opened a door with a nameplate conspicuously missing, and handed her the key. Shyly, they stood there until she thanked them and shut the door. She placed her wood and brass nameplate on the desk and began to make order of the papers littered there.

Tribal Chairman Ezra Bangs The Drum came to see her around 10:30. He silently approved of the sorted paper stacks his new controller was creating to fill the time. "Your accountant, Bob Wilson, has a personal day today. He'll be in tomorrow and will be invaluable to you."

"All due respect, Mr. Bangs The Drum, but today would have been invaluable." With her characteristic manner of getting right to the point, she asked, "Is there a problem with Bob Wilson?"

Her boss chuckled. This woman was going to do just fine. "He wanted the job, of course. With our many holdings, we require a CPA, which he isn't. He's been here six years, and I believe he'll come around, Miz Carver.

"Now," he continued, "I'll take you around and introduce you to everyone. Then I will take you to lunch. And then I expect you'll have your work cut out for you from now until calendar year's end."

In the accounting office, the chairman introduced Tally to each of the clerks and to Marian Moses, her personal assistant. "I'll ask you later what you do for me, Marian," she said, and smiled at the group. "For now, I'd like to have a staff meeting in the conference room—do we have a conference room?—at 1:30, so please schedule your lunches to be back by then."

She went on the tour with Ezra, meeting about twenty-five other tribal employees in the building. Then they went to the Poplar Café. Blue Cloud waited on them.

"This is Miz Carver," Ezra introduced her. "She's our new controller."

"Nice to see you again, Ms. Carver." Blue Cloud smiled. "Great beef stew in a sourdough bowl on special today, $5.50 with salad." It came quickly, and they were eating silently when Gerry Marsden intruded.

"May I?" He stood by politely.

Tally looked quizzically at him. Surely, he realized this was her first business lunch with the Tribal Chairman. She waited for Ezra to reinforce that notion and was surprised to hear the chairman ask Valu-Wear's general manager to join them.

Gerry moved carefully into Ezra's side of the booth, facing Tally across the scarred and varnished wood of the tabletop. "Ms. Carver, how nice to see you again. Is old Ezra here treatin' you okay?"

They finished their lunches to light conversation. Tally and her boss left Gerry in the booth, and Tally noticed that Ezra paid Gerry's lunch ticket, also. Ezra was even more impressed with Tally when she responded to his query as to whether he should come to her staff meeting.

"No, sir. Your time is too valuable to waste on clerical issues. I'll call on you for help with important decisions, okay?" Tally was good at her work. She was in charge of her department, even if this was the first day.

The meeting was informational, the staff friendly, and Marian Moses was certainly going to be invaluable. She would wait to find out on Tuesday whether that was the case with Bob Wilson. A weary Tally locked her office door late Monday afternoon, after the accounting office was empty of personnel. A good first day, she thought.

A knocking sounded at her locked screen door at seven that evening. Her heart lifted at the sound, and she ran her fingers hurriedly through her hair in the hallway. She brushed at the closet dust on the front of her navy blue sweat pants, and went casually to the door. Gerry Marsden stood there.

"I come bearing gifts." A gift bag was in one hand, a bottle of California Zinfandel in the other. Southern-bred hostess that she was, Tally did not show her disappointment at the identity of her visitor.

He'd been planning this, she realized, as she took the wine from him. It was chilled and ready to drink. Gerry took a corkscrew from the breast pocket of his striped casual shirt. "Do you have glasses unpacked yet, Tally?" He was opening the wine without waiting for her reply.

Two wedding gift goblets appeared from the top shelf of a kitchen cupboard, and they carried their wine into the living room. Gerry placed the bottle on the bamboo coffee table. "Official 'welcome' to Fort Peck, Tally," he said, and placed the lightweight gift in her lap. She lifted away the tissue paper in its top as he uncorked the wine.

"Ooh! Oh, Gerry," she squealed with delight. "It's one of those Assiniboine Stars I saw in the gift shop Friday. Oh, what a treat." She removed the large sofa pillow from the bag and pressed her cheek to it. "Oh, it is so wonderful. Thank you so much."

"Aw, shucks, ma'am," he drawled playfully. "It ain't nothin'."

"I'll have to put it on my bed, Gerry, because it doesn't go with the couch, but it will be great against my blue duvet." She hugged it again and set it at her feet to sip at her wine.

He dropped the drawl for a serious tone. "No place I'd rather you keep it, Tally. On your bed is just fine." There was an instant, Tally knew, when she could have leaned forward and been kissed. She let the moment pass and sipped her Zinfandel again.

They made a date for dinner Friday night. "We'll go early, Tally, so it will still be light," Gerry said. "And you can see Wolf Point. It's quite a famous little town in rodeo circles. The Wolf Point Stampede, you know."

They chatted about her work. She asked him if he knew Bob Wilson. He lived in Glasgow with his wife and a couple of children, Gerry told her, then asked, "Is there a problem with him?"

"Well, I don't know. He took a personal day today. He's my number one guy, you know, so I thought he should have been there. Or at least lied and called in sick!" She chuckled a little.

"Best thing to do, Tally, is get 'em to resign and bring in your own crew. Especially if they're going to give you problems." He nodded his head sagely and refilled their wineglasses.

She laughed. "Well, that's not been my management style to date, Gerry, but I'll keep it in mind. Right now, I have to look over some papers and get ready for tomorrow, so I'm throwing you out."

He went without protest, patting her cheek as she stood with him a moment at the door. My, he *was* good-looking, she told herself, as she once again let the moment pass. Gerry went silently down the stairs to his own apartment.

Bob Wilson presented himself at her office door at 8:25 on Tuesday morning. He was about thirty-five. His sandy hair had cowlicks at the crown, and he looked comfortable in a cord sport coat over blue jeans. She looked pointedly at her Seiko before she shook hands with him. "What are your regular hours, Bob, so I'll know when I can expect to be here with you?"

"Ms. Carver, I've had mostly flex time as long as I got my work done. I come in long hours at years' end. I work shorter weeks in mid-quarters the rest of the year. It works out."

"I'm in favor of flex time in our profession, Bob. But for June and July, I'd like you to be here with me while I'm learning the lay of the land. Is eight to five good, or eight-thirty to five-thirty? Pick one, and I'll count on it. Now, I have a question about the Accounts Payable, so I'd like you to get the aging and explain these amounts to me." She reached in her briefcase and read off a short series of numbers. He was impassive as he responded.

"Sarah Grey Wolf is the Accounts Payable clerk, Ms. Carver. Perhaps you should talk with her." His tone was not disrespectful. It was bored.

"You have an accounting degree, Bob? Yes? I thought so. You are, indeed, our accountant? Yep, thought so again." She was controlled, but angry. "Am I out of line to think that you would be on top of anything the accounting staff prepares?"

He mumbled and told of special projects for the Board taking his time. "Okay, Bob. Each staff member is giving me a list by 3 PM today. A list of their responsibilities daily, weekly, monthly, quarterly, and annually. I'll have to ask you to do the same for me. Please list the extra projects you're doing for the Board, and when they're due."

He grew more attentive, as she grew more forceful. "Do you want the Accounts Payable thing first, Ms. Carver?"

"Yes, I do. Get with Sarah if you have to, and bring me the answers this morning. And, Bob, please call me Tally. If you sign paychecks, you'll note that is not my given name. Do not—I repeat—*do not* feel free to call me Thalia." Her eyes had been sharp and grayed, and they now softened with blue as she laughed at her joke.

Bob Wilson laughed a little with her and left grudgingly to do some real accounting. His free ride is going to be over, she said to herself as he went into his office across the hall. That's his problem with me. And not getting this job, of course.

At lunchtime, she ate half a sandwich and an apple at her desk, while paging through the sheets of computer paper Bob had handed her when he answered her Accounts Payable questions. Her watch said three o'clock when she next looked at it. She stood, stretched, and opened her door.

Marian Moses was in the hallway, three other clerks behind her. Each had their lists in their hands. Chairs scraped in the outer office as the others hurried to turn in their schedule of duties. "Thanks, all." She smiled and waved them single-file through her small office. "I'll be talking to you later." As the last clerk disappeared around the corner, Tally noticed a familiar form standing in the doorway to Bob Wilson's office.

The voice that had been haunting her daydreams was speaking. "Okay, Mr. Wilson. Where is her office, then?" Joshua spoke formally for the benefit of listening ears, the ever-present moccasin telegraph. He turned at Bob's instruction and locked eyes with Tally. Those eyes are steely gray today, he thought. Wonder if that means all business?

"Ms. Carver? Joshua Smith. I picked you up at the airport? May I speak with you for a minute?"

She signaled him into her office, where he closed the door and stood facing her. "Nice to see you again, Tally Jo Carver, even if it's on business. Shall we do business first?"

Tally was never flustered at work. She was an expert, a precise business manager and accountant. Her color grew high, however, and her voice was almost shaky as she answered him. "Uh, business, of course, Joshua." *Damn! It's that sweet grass fragrance again. It makes me nuts.*

"Your accountant has acquired an attitude, Tally. Against you, I'm afraid. I've always gone to him when the Tribe was late paying one of my bills. Fifteen days, that's my deal. I'm a little guy. At twenty days, I'm in here for the money. He sends me to you, says you want to be in charge of Accounts Payable. I don't want all that information, Tally. Just my check."

"This is my first day with him, Joshua." She shrugged her shoulders and looked sad as she replied, "I think I can win him over. For now, let's see about getting your money." She stood to go to the outer office.

"Hold it, Tally. Don't know about the accounting business, but I know a lot about the people business. He will lay siege if you give him the opportunity. Why not make your stand right here?" He stood there, silent, while her brain worked.

He had put his hand on her wrist when she moved to open the door. His touch was light, yet she could not turn the knob. She was mesmerized as he spoke again. "If you folks pay me, Tally, I would buy enough gas to take you exploring this weekend. Maybe even stand you to an Indian taco. I hear you're particularly fond of them." His smile caused her toes to tingle.

Why, Joshua Dale Smith. She was astonished, perceptive. We're not so different. You make a little joke when some-

thing feels serious. "I'll ask you about tacos later, Joshua. But, yes, I'd like to go into the countryside this weekend. Early?"

They decided on nine o'clock Saturday morning. She walked him across the accounting office to the tiny lobby and asked him to wait. Then she went to Bob's open office door. "Bob?" Tally's voice was friendly. "Bring those two hand ledgers and come into my office." She gestured at the books on his desk. "Now, please."

He sat in her office, confused. She didn't even know what was in the books he'd carried across the hall. "Bob," she explained, "the ledgers are an excuse. So that staff won't know I am chewing you out. This is, I hope, the only time I have to yell at my right-hand man. What makes you think finding a check for a supplier is in my job description? Especially since we just spoke about you being the overseer of Accounts Payable?"

He hung his head for a moment. When he looked up, his eyes were sincere. "I'm sorry. Could we start over again, Tally?"

Her first week passed in a blur of numbers, playing catch-up with financial reports due and past due to the Tribal Board. Gerry was waiting for her when she came home from work on Wednesday, after six.

"You look beat, Miss Tally," he began. "Why don't we run into Wolf Point for dinner? Have a drink, relax, and you won't have to cook." He was standing in front of the stairs.

"Beat isn't the word, Gerry. I'm too tired to wash my face, and too hateful to be good company. I'll get my act together before Friday night, I promise. But not tonight, okay?"

"I know it seems like I'm rushing you, Tally. I'm sorry. But my vacation is scheduled—my kids are expecting me, and I fly out of Billings Saturday morning. I'll be gone all next week. I just hoped to get to know you better before I left." His handsome face was contrite.

"No problem, Gerry," she answered, as she started past him up the stairs. I should ask him up for a glass of his wine, she thought. But he is kind of...pushy.

Friday at five, Bob Wilson stuck his head in her open door. "Need me for anything, boss lady?" He'd been helpful and courteous all week. "My daughter has summer softball and her first game is at six, in Glasgow."

"You go, Bob. I'm leaving now, too." She got up from her desk, took his right hand, put her left hand on top of their handclasp.

"We've done good work this week, Bob. I appreciate your turn-around, and I appreciate you. Thanks." She patted and released his hand. He shrugged his shoulders and looked relieved. The clerks looked at one another with soft smiles as he bade them a cheery goodnight.

She wore blue gingham culottes with a matching sleeveless blouse and strappy sandals on her bare legs. One drop of perfume, and she was ready to go when Gerry knocked at her door. She grabbed a white knit stole to ward off the cool June evening. "Could we go to a movie, Gerry?"

"That'd be in Glasgow, Tally. But there is a really good restaurant there. Yes, we could do that." He was courteously handing her into his late-model Cadillac.

"Good! How big is Glasgow?"

"I don't know, Tally. I'd say about six thousand. It isn't on the reservation. Nice little Montana town. I make a trip about once a month to the supermarket there. We could go together, if you'd like that."

They talked comfortably all the way to the restaurant. She had a whiskey sour and ate her first wall-eyed pike at his suggestion. Battered and crisp, it was the best fish she had ever tasted. "Oh, look, I've devoured everything but the wall-eyes themselves!" They enjoyed dinner.

"No time for after-dinner drinks, Tally, if you're sure we still want to go to the movie." Gerry leaned over the table and covered her hand. "Or would you rather just have some drinks and dance, or something?"

"Forgot to tell you, Gerry. I hate to dance. I'll do it if I have to, but I dislike dancing. Intensely. And I really love movies. Good, bad, long, short—I love 'em. Let's go to the movie, okay?" She didn't let her slight anger show. A movie date is a movie date, she thought.

After a stilted start, Tally and Gerry had a fine time. They made incredulous eyes at one another over some of the dialogue in the second run action movie they saw. They giggled when their hands collided in the round popcorn box. Exiting the theater, Gerry confessed. "I didn't really want to go to the movies, Tally. But it's sure fun to see one with you. It's only ten-thirty—should we have a nightcap?"

"Not tonight, Gerry. Really long week, and I'm dead tired. And you have to pack and go to the airport at six in the morning! You need your beauty sleep, too." They headed back to Poplar.

At her door, he had one more suggestion. "A glass of wine before we say goodnight?" His hand was on the screen door.

She sidestepped neatly. "I'm too full of popcorn and bonbons, Gerry. Thanks so much for my first Montana movie. I had a good time." He leaned down, found no resistance, and kissed her.

His lips were firm, insistent. The aura of his aftershave was pleasant, and Tally relaxed and enjoyed her first kiss in months. His tongue penetrated her soft underlip and explored a moment. When there was no reciprocation, he ended the kiss immediately.

"Wonderful, Tally. Just wonderful. Thanks for the evening. I can't wait to get back from Connecticut." He stood at the door and waited until she was inside before he strolled down the stairs.

She lingered inside the kitchen door and sorrowed when she could not detect the smell of sweet grass. Resolutely, she walked through the dark rooms to the bathroom. There she took a long, hot shower, scrubbing furiously to rid herself of Obsession and any trace of English Leather.

CHAPTER FIVE

Her heart was racing like a teenager's on her first date when she opened the door to Joshua the next morning. It was exactly nine o'clock.

"How do you know about me and Indian tacos?" Tally quizzed him before he was even in the kitchen. She was dressed casually in blue jeans and a pale blue, sleeveless shirt, its collar showing above the crew neck of her navy blue sweatshirt, and she was sans Obsession.

He smiled sweetly. "Moccasin telegraph, Miz Tally." At her quizzical look, he explained. "That's what we call gossip on the reservation, Tally. Stuff spreads from person to person faster than by telegraph. Blue Cloud is a kind of cousin of mine. She mentioned that she met you." *Mentioned that you were too good for that stuck-up snob, Marsden, is what she mentioned.* He did not voice this thought, but continued smiling.

His boots were black today and polished to a high gloss, she noticed. She longed to touch his thick, blue-black hair. It hung freely, not in the stubby ponytail she remembered. He wore jeans and a small-patterned cowboy shirt with pearl snaps, and a small medicine bag hung around his neck. *He is* truly copper colored, thought Tally. I wonder how much of that is from working outside?

"Am I dressed properly for the tour you have in mind, Joshua?" She pirouetted slowly.

He looked skeptically at her Adidas running shoes. "Do you have boots? Hiking boots, not those high-heeled ones you were wearing with the riding skirt. We're well-known for rattlesnakes in Montana, you know."

"Could we buy some before we head into the country, Joshua? In Wolf Point, maybe?"

"Rattlesnakes, Tally, or boots?" He favored her with that inscrutable smile again and said it wouldn't be out of the way. On the way downstairs, he looked at Gerry's apartment door and said, "The shoe man is gone for a week, huh?"

"How did you—" Tally began, and then realized that Joshua surely knew she'd been out with Gerry just last night. "Oh, moccasin telegraph again, I guess?"

She was delighted with his ten-year-old Jeep, its panels open to the Montana morning. He inquired about her work as the drive began, and her relationship with Bob Wilson. "Knew you'd get that handled in a right manner, Tally," he complimented her. "And thanks to Bob and the Tribe's check," he gestured expansively around the Jeep's interior," I can escort you about today in all this luxury!"

"Are there any mountains around here at all, Joshua?" Tally was eyeing the blue-domed, flat world again. "Now I know how those early explorers felt, when they thought they'd fall off the edge of the world. It looks like it, doesn't it?"

He explained that there were just some rocky hills scattered about, debris left behind when the last glaciers scraped over this part of the country. She watched him as he spoke of the Montana landscape. It's as if he were praying, she thought. He loves this land, that's for sure.

They parked in front of the western haberdashery in Wolf Point. "It's a tourist trap," Joshua warned, "but they have nice boots."

They entered the store. The smell of new wool and leather was pleasant in the air. An aging man came to wait on them. "Yes, ma'am? May I help you?" To Joshua, who was just behind Tally, the clerk said, "I'll be with you after a while," and turned his body wholly to the woman.

Joshua's face was impassive. Tally didn't hesitate. "That's okay, we're together," she trilled and took Joshua's arm. "You weren't going to look at anything anyway, were you, Josh? I want work boots—hiking boots, you know?" Still clinging to Joshua, she propelled him along with her behind the clerk.

Joshua's face was stern. The clerk was in the back getting three pairs of boots for Tally to try.

"You okay?" Her concern was visible as she looked at his storm-cloud face again.

He leaned over and spoke tenderly in her ear. "Thalia. Don't…call…me…Josh. Ever. Okay?"

Her laughter pealed. "I guess that was overdoing it a bit, huh? I just didn't like his attitude, but I loved the boots in the window." The man was returning, and Joshua hurried to finish the conversation.

"You'll meet with some bigotry, Tally, if we're going to see each other. It will come from both sides. Ezra Bangs The Drum is a good man. You could talk to him about it."

Her heart sang as they continued on the highway. "See each other," he'd said. *See each other.* Whoopee! He's thinking about "seeing each other!"

"Where are we going first, Joshua?" Tally spoke modest-ly, not betraying the song in her heart. "Aren't we close to the edge of the reservation?"

"Going to show you where they're starting to set up for Red Bottom Days, out near Frazer, Tally. It's the Assiniboine annual powwow celebration. Weekend after next. They're starting to clean up now, set up teepee poles, make the brush circles for the dancing competitions. You won't recognize it on the actual weekend, the little valley will be so covered in teepee lodges and stands and people."

He was silent for a few miles, and she watched the un-changing roadside.

"Then we'll go back to Wolf Point and cut up toward Scobey," he continued. "Two hundred acres of my land is there. It's part of the Wooden Headdress ranch—my grand-father is Raymond Wooden Headdress—and there's a cave I'd like to look for, there on Square Butte. I haven't seen it for twenty-five years." Am I bragging to her, showing off about my land? Grandfathers, is this too soon? My heart is so sure. Could you give me a sign?

An enthusiastic crew of twenty Indian people was do-ing the cleanup of the Red Bottom grounds that Joshua had described. Most were middle-aged. A few children played on the edges of the work sites. Several teenagers worked along-side their elders, three or four of them definitely disgruntled at the day's occupation. "Kids today, Tally. White or black or Indian. Chinese and stuff, too, for all I know. They're losing respect for tradition, for their elders.

"Yet if these kids live past drug abuse and alcoholism and fast cars and mean tempers, Red Bottom Days and this work here will be among their finest memories." He slumped, head against the steering wheel. Tally began to reach for him, then intuitively knew she should not. When he sat up straight again, Joshua finished his commentary.

"They are mine. Best memories. I was off-reservation for nine years. Those are the worst memories of my life. The good memories kept me alive, brought me home. Tally, I pray each day that my son and daughter will benefit from my hard-won wisdom."

They sat there, silent, in the Jeep at the side of the old road. Joshua was deep in thought about the terrible years when he was away. Tally wondered where his wife was, how old his children were, why didn't she suspect that a wonderful man like this one was already taken? The cleanup crew folks talked among themselves about lunch, looking at their watches. Montana's fierce sun climbed toward the top of its cloudless dome, raining brilliance on all.

On the road again, Joshua said, "I think we'll have lunch a little early, Tally. Best place in this part of the country is right…about…here." He pulled into a big gravel parking lot as he finished his sentence. A log building that looked like an old-time saloon, complete with hitching posts, sat at the rear of the parking area.

"Beer, Tally?" Joshua asked as the waitress requested their drink orders.

"Yeah, I think that'd be good for the dust, since I'm not the driver. Draft, please."

He ordered a tall lemonade, lots of ice. "Driving a precious cargo, you see," he twinkled, as he raised his glass at her.

She wondered if he was flirting. No, she thought, this Joshua Dale Smith doesn't flirt. Oh, my, what am I getting into?

They decided on western steak sandwiches with steak fries and coleslaw, and talked about her work and the division of Sioux and Assiniboine that made up the Fort Peck Tribes until the food came. Finally, she could stand it no longer. When the waitress had served all the food, Tally fixed him with her gaze and got to the point.

"Explain please, Joshua. About 'seeing each other.' What does that mean, 'seeing each other'?"

He was carefully cutting a large French fry into fork-sized pieces. He placed a bite into his mouth and chewed it slowly, not taking his eyes from her face. He swallowed. "This, Tally." He gestured around them, his black eyes luminous. "You and I. Being together. This is 'seeing each other,' isn't it?"

"Of course. Dating, you mean. This is…dating…isn't it? We are…on a date…aren't we?"

"It's going to be whatever you want it to be, Tally. Why don't we just let it happen? Seeing each other." He picked up half his sandwich and took a large bite, signaling an end to the conversation.

Tally wasn't through. "But what about…um…your family, Joshua? Do you live with them?"

He placed the sandwich back on his plate, chewed carefully and wiped his mouth deliberately. The napkin went back into his lap. "Tally, darlin', I'll tell you anything you want to know, but I didn't have breakfast. Could I eat before you begin a lifetime of nagging me?"

She picked up a French fry, and then attacked her sandwich. *Nagging. A lifetime of nagging. He called me darlin'. My God, what's happening to me? I am giddy, ready to fall into this man's arms. After he has his lunch, of course.* She giggled at the thought. He looked up from his plate and did not speak.

I have nothing to judge by, she thought. But that has to be pure love light shining from his eyes. It is. It's brother and lover and protector and friend, all rolled into one. Would it last a long lifetime, I wonder?

The dusty Jeep retraced their route and headed back to Wolf Point. "I wanted you to see the Red Bottom site, Tally," Joshua explained. "So you'd know where it was, and know what people were talking about. It's a big deal to the Assiniboine half of the Fort Peck Tribes. It was started a hundred years ago by the Red Bottom Clan, of which I am directly descended through my mother.

"My mother was full blood. My father was white, gone before I was born. That makes me a half-breed. Not a bad name like it was a hundred years ago. Only about 20% of the Tribe is of full blood anymore.

"We'll check in at the ranch house with my sister, Rosie, before we go up to Square Butte. She's seven years older than I am, and had a different white father. She's a widow and runs Grandpa's ranch with an iron fist."

Joshua finished explaining. "Wait 'til we get out of this Jeep, Tally. Up at Square Butte. Then I'll tell you anything you want to know. Deal?"

He steadied the wheel with his left hand and reached over to cup her cheek with the other. She could not resist turning her head to nestle into his hand, placing the merest butterfly kiss in its palm. He brought the hand back to his own lips and, for a moment, she thought she would weep.

They rode in silence past rangeland dotted with horses and cattle and an occasional capped oil well, its teeter-totter arms moving to a slow dance beat. Joshua turned the Jeep into the well-maintained driveway of a large, white farmhouse with many red outbuildings. A white picket fence that needed paint surrounded the front of the house. Some irises were in bud, tulips and daffodils nearly done blooming.

Rosie Smith Elk Horn stood on the other side of the screen door. She was shorter than Tally, and lean, bronzed as much from outdoor work as from her heritage. She peered through the screen, shading her eyes against the one o'clock sun. Recognizing Joshua, Rosie snorted to hide her joy.

"Hmmph!" Rosie loved her little brother more than anything—more than the ranch, more than their grandfather, more than the tribal politics in which she was deeply involved. She was sure his return to the reservation three years ago was a direct answer to her ten years of prayer. "Hmmph! Thought you'd died or somethin'."

"Rosie, this is Tally Carver. She's the Tribe's new controller, in charge of the bookkeeping over there. We're going to take the Jeep up to Square Butte, okay?"

"You Indian, Tally?" Rosie was blunt. There were pale-eyed tribal members on all reservations in this day and age.

"No, I'm not. I'm English and Welsh, I'm told." Tally was sweetly polite and not defensive, although this little woman was surely formidable. "Nice to have met you, Rosie," she said, as they turned to go back to the Jeep.

Rosie motioned for Joshua to come back and spoke to him through the screen door. "What's with this girl, my brother?"

"Aw, Rosie. Don't be a bigot. A reverse bigot. This is a wonderful woman, Sister. She lifts the tears from my heart and sets them to music. Would I take just anyone up to Square Butte?"

Rosie pondered, stubborn for just a moment before her love for him won out. "Stop by the house for a cool drink on your way back, Joshua, okay?"

Beyond the huge barn, Square Butte seemed to be a stone's throw away. "It's about three miles," he told her. There was a rough trail for about a mile. "For branding," Joshua explained. Then the Jeep was on its own, carving a path into cropped grass dotted with rocks and gopher holes, crossing a small creek when nearly there. The going was rough, and conversation halted.

It loomed above them, about two hundred feet. The last glacier had probably carved and left it to stand sentinel on the surrounding land. Bushes grew at its base and greenery was sparse on its rocky way to the butte's flat tabletop. "We need to hike around to the west side, Tally. New boots up to it?" He helped her from the Jeep.

Tally was fit from isometrics and from running whenever she could. She could tell he approved of the resolved way she attacked the hostile landscape. Her happiness cup overflowed when she saw the pride on his face as she matched his progress.

The view of the other side of Square Butte was different. It turned in upon itself, and large rocks tumbled about. Some skinny cottonwoods were in nearly full leaf, centered at the bottom. Joshua guided her toward them. Several two-ton boulders about four feet high had created a haphazard, miniature Stonehenge.

They sat on opposing rocks in the small enclosure. The trees rustled prettily, but gave no shade against the sun. The natural benches they sat upon were warm, and Tally took off her sweatshirt. "Okay, Tally," he said. "Ask me anything."

She looked at him for an eternity, certain she was in love with this stranger. What should she ask? What did she want to know other than when would he kiss her? Did anything or anyone else matter when they were together?

"Um, yeah. Where's the cave, Joshua? We're burnin' day-light!" she joked, her heart too full to speak of other things.

They couldn't find the cave he had last seen twenty-five years ago, and which his grandfather had discovered fifty years before that. He explained that one of Montana's few earthquakes had crumbled Square Butte's restless founda-tion, and the cave probably filled up with rock. In a dark crevice grew a solitary pale purple flower, which he picked and offered to her.

"Pasque flower, Tally. Probably the last one of spring. They've been gone from the prairie for weeks. For you." She tucked it in her headband for protection as they climbed down the butte and hiked out to the Jeep. On the ground, she removed and held it tenderly. It was already beginning to wither, and she shivered in the sunshine.

"Rosie asked us to stop and have a cold drink. Okay?"

"Oh, Joshua." Tally tried to be circumspect. "It's already 2:30. Don't we have a lot more to see?" She doesn't like me, is rude to me, and I don't want to go into her house.

It was as if he heard her thoughts. "She'll be okay, Tally. She made up her mind when she asked us in. She's my el-der sister, and I don't want to refuse her. Please?" He wasn't pleading, she knew. The "please" was a concession.

Rosie Elk Horn had homemade lemonade for them in a tall, cut glass pitcher. The glistening glass sang as ice cubes bounced against it when the brown, wiry woman poured the tart drink. Oreo cookies were stacked on a flowered plate. Once again, she got to the point. "The kids know you two are goin' together, Joshua Dale?"

Tally sputtered on her lemonade. "Ah, Rosie, we...we aren't..."

Seated next to her on the sofa in Rosie's crowded parlor, Joshua was resigned. He patted her free hand.

"Tally. Probably we are." He turned back to Rosie. "No. I'll tell them tonight when I take them to supper. Christy and Jo Ellen, too. Before the moccasin telegraph gets to them. Thanks for the reminder, Sister."

Probably we're "going together?" He will tell the kids tonight? Christy? Jo Ellen? She put on a calm face as exciting thoughts raced through her brain. Tell them what, exactly?

Brother and sister chatted away about the ranch and their grandfather. Rosie drew Tally into the conversation, asking her how she liked her work so far. Joshua stood up to go after fifteen minutes had elapsed.

His sister hurried into the next room and came back with a bundle under her arm and a beaded key chain that she handed to Joshua. She partially unfolded the bundle she held out to Tally. "Thank you for coming to my home," she intoned. "May this star quilt bless yours, always."

Tally was overwhelmed, but thanked Rosie in the same, solemn manner. The quilt was multicolored on an eggshell background, different sizes of Assiniboine Stars surrounding a large one. She lay her cheek against it lovingly as she said good-bye to the older woman.

In the Jeep on the quiet road to Poplar, Tally carried on about her surprise at such a luxurious gift. Joshua explained. "My sister is traditional. She says she has never had a problem with her white blood, that she made up her mind when she was nine years old that she was an Indian. Traditional Indians gift you when you visit them. Although..." Joshua chuckled here, "...I don't think she's ever given a star quilt to a white girl before!"

Tally's eyes had traveled to a scene near the river. Several elderly women were alighting from two cars parked nearly in the ditch beside another at the side of the narrow road. Each carried a round, flat-bottomed wicker basket. Beyond the ditch and away from the river sat a small makeshift hut in front of a waving grass field, where another woman seemed to be tending a small fire. The basket-carriers headed in that direction.

"Joshua, what's going on there? Can we stop? I'd like to see those baskets."

"We cannot stop and should avert our eyes, Tally." Joshua made his jeep creep past the parked cars, studiously studying the road ahead. When he rounded the first curve in the bumpy road, he pulled over and stopped. "Those grandmothers are gathering the sweet grass, Tally. It's an annual ritual. They will take a dust-off sweat in the portable sweat lodge to rid themselves of the nuisances of the world, and will be in prayer for the people for whom the sweet grass is intended. Then they will go into the field and harvest. It's a special time, a special job for the People. And very private.

"I just have time to show you where I live." He changed the subject in the twinkling of an eye. "In case you ever want to find me nights or weekends?" He gave her that smile again. "I don't have a phone out there."

He was well aware of the beauty of his home site along the river, but was delighted to hear her gasp as they dropped down onto his corduroy road from the secondary gravel. Birch, cottonwood, and weeping willow lined the riverbank and surrounded the leveled area above. His small, silver-bullet trailer was incongruous in the center of the clearing. The Ford flatbed sat in front of the trailer, a blue tarp covering the mysterious lumps and bumps of its cargo. Mazurka nickered from her lush spot by the river as they got out of the Jeep.

"This is forty acres, Tally. Also my inherited land. I'll build here one day." Yes, he thought, I'm showing off my holdings. I'll be offering Ezra many ponies by this time next week!

She exclaimed at the beauty of the setting as they walked to the raw wooden platform that served as entry to his front door. "Engineer! It's okay, boy. C'mon out!" As the big black and tan dog bounded from under the trailer, Joshua explained.

"He always does that when someone new comes. Waiting to see if they're a threat to the place, I think. Good boy, good Engineer!" He patted the dog absently and opened the unlocked trailer door. "Want to wait in here while I get my filly and bring her up for the night? Or go with me?"

Tally opted for "go with," of course. She did not want to leave his side. She was anxious to learn if "going together" was more committed than "seeing each other."

He took her hand as she descended the three steps and did not release it while they strolled slowly toward the river and Mazurka. He nearly gave her the filly when she squealed with delight at a Mazurka-kiss. When his four-legged friends were both feasting on evening rations, Joshua Dale Smith climbed his steps once more. He held out his hand and said, "Come, Tally. I'll show you my home."

Chapter Six

It was an old travel trailer with solid wood panelling and cupboards. The fragrance of sweet grass was overpowering. "Here, I'll leave the door open and air it out a little," he offered.

"Oh, no," she breathed. "I love it. I'd never smelled it before, but already I like it more than perfume."

He nodded. He'd noticed right away that she was wearing only soap today.

She saw he was neat. His coffeepot was on the propane stove. A cup with some coffee dregs sat on the small Formica kitchen table. A cozy, wood-armed couch snugged into the river end of the trailer and the large, curved window above it provided a spectacular view of the shallow, willow-lined Poplar. On the low table in front of the couch sat a heavy wood bowl with ashes in it. A half-burnt braid of sweet grass lay across the bowl. Next to it lay a piece of soft, tanned leather that looked to Tally like a chamois skin. Two metal tools lay on top of the leather.

She sat down on the couch. A few books were stacked on a small desk. From her vantage point, she could see to the other end of the trailer. Bathroom and closet were in the middle, she guessed. Tiny, tiny bedroom in back. His bed was rumpled.

"Should I warm up this coffee, Tally?" Joshua was looking in his little built-in refrigerator. "Or something cold? A can of lemon tea?"

She opted for the tea. He took one himself, and sat at a padded stool at his kitchen table. "I just wanted you to see where I am, Tally. I like to imagine where the person is if I'm thinking of them, or talking to them on the phone. And I wanted you to meet my animals." He sat and sipped his tea in silence. After a moment, he began to speak.

"My kids are James-Dale, fifteen, and Ellen Joy, fourteen. They live in Poplar with their mother's mother, Jo Ellen Warbonnet Red Leggins, and their aunt, Christy…" Joshua went on, telling her the story in as few words as he could. He finished with, "I've had no woman since I returned to the reservation three years ago," and looked at her.

She didn't know what to say. It was so sad. Childhood sweethearts, just kids themselves. "If it's okay to ask," she began, "are your children all right about your return?"

He shrugged his shoulders. "I'm thirty-five at the end of the month, Tally. I was away from the kids for nine years. They have a settled existence with their aunt and grandmother. I will spend the next thirty-five years making up for the first thirty-five, I guess. There's an old hawk who hunts from a cottonwood snag you can see out this window here. I have a kindred spirit with that hawk. Both of us alone. I say hello to him every evening." He peered out at the lengthening shadows. "He should be coming back to his tree about now. Take a look out here, Tally. Straight out, then about 30 degrees left."

He moved his stool back so she could stand next to the table and bend down to peer out the window. Unaccustomed to the terrain, she had not yet located the tree when Joshua gasped over her shoulder. Then her eyes lit on the dying cottonwood. Two hawks sat on the topmost bare branch.

Thank you for the sign, Grandfathers. Thank you. He took her shoulders firmly and slowly turned her around. "Tally, I'm going to kiss you now."

She couldn't think, much less make a joke, when the eons-long kiss ended. Tears hovered at the corners of her eyes and tiny chills descended from her scalp to her bare shoulders. She wavered, her motion tipping the stool to the floor. Joshua steadied her, his strong arms wrapped tightly around her.

With her head on his shoulder, he rocked her slowly. "There, there," he crooned, then separated their bodies without embarrassment. He lowered her tenderly to the remaining upright stool and stood, smoothing her hair away from her face with the palms of both callused hands. One gentle finger traced the moisture beneath her left eye.

"Dark blue, now," he mused aloud. "Strange eyes you have, dear girl. Now, is there still a question about our 'going together?' Or will I be forced to kiss you again before the shoe man gets back?"

"No, of course not," she stammered. "I mean—of course, you will. I mean—oh, Joshua!" She shook her head back and forth in confusion, accidentally dislodging his hands. He placed them on each side of her face again, firmly, and bent to place the sweetest of kisses on her swollen mouth.

"Of course, I will," he repeated. "Of course." He helped her gently to her feet. "We must go now, dear one. My children expect me to take them to supper shortly. And I'll be telling them and their grandmother—who isn't named Warbonnet for nothing!—and their aunt that I am 'going with' Tally Jo Carver. Right?" He peered at her flushed face and nodded sagely. "Right."

He gave her a little push on the fanny, and she took a couple of steps toward the trailer's door. Then he reached into the cupboard she had been standing beneath and brought down a braid of sweet grass about ten inches long. "Thank you for coming to my home." His tone was formal as he handed it to her.

She had to go? She couldn't believe it. But Tally took the braid of grass gratefully, passing it under her nostrils and breathing in the odor that had been haunting her. "Thank you, Joshua Dale. I'll put it in my car. Or is that all right?" She was afraid she'd do or say something to ruin one of these perfect moments.

He pushed her, none too gently, toward the door he was opening. "All right, if that's where you want it, girl. It's for safety, the scent of prayer. It'll work anywhere, I guess. Let's get going now, okay?"

He bade the shepherd to stay and guard, and they were off once again in the Jeep. Tally was still reeling from the entreating passion of Joshua's first kiss, and they were silent during the fifteen minutes it took to get to Tally's apartment building.

A chunky young Indian woman was sweeping the cement walkway in front of her ground floor apartment as they got out of the vehicle. "O-ho, Candy," Joshua addressed her, as they stood at the bottom of the steps that rose above her.

"Hi ya, Joshua," the sweeper replied, eyes still on the broom and dustpan she was using.

"Have you met your new neighbor?" Joshua's question was rhetorical. Tally had already mentioned she'd seen no one but Gerry Marsden at her apartment building.

"Candy St. Albans, this is Tally Carver. Tally, Candy. Tally's the new controller at the Tribe, Candy. And Candy works at the shoe factory and lives here with her little boy. What's his name again, Candy?"

"It's Jerome. He's three." She almost smiled with this last information, shyly, in Tally's direction. "Nice to meet you," she said, as she continued pushing dust and grass clippings into her dustpan.

Up the stairs at Tally's door, Joshua leaned in to her as she inserted her key in the lock. "Everyone will be wondering about our relationship, dear girl. We can't disappoint anyone who's watching." He held and hugged her for a long minute, leaving a lover's kiss on the side of her neck.

He grinned. "That should satisfy them." He held her at arm's length and looked her up and down. His grin ended in a sigh. "Can't say the same for this ol' indun, though!" He was comically sad as he turned to go.

"Will I see you tomorrow, Joshua? Would you like to come for breakfast?" She was afraid she sounded needy, but didn't want to spend a weekend day without at least the sight of him. "Or lunch?"

"I have lunch with my grandfather, Raymond Wooden Headdress. Most every Sunday, here in Poplar. He's ninety-three. Are you ready to come with me, meet him, hear about the little brown boy I was? I'd like to take you."

He turned to leave. Joshua didn't want to seem too eager and didn't want her to see his disappointment if she didn't want to go with him.

Her voice trembled as she replied. "Joshua, I'm a strong woman, used to taking charge of my own life. But I'm so scared I'll do something wrong here—with you—and mess this thing up, whatever it's going to be. So why don't you be in charge of the parts that are familiar to you? You were right about your sister, you see. So I'll go if you think it's right. Otherwise, some other Sunday would be fine. Okay?"

He stepped back and faced her as she stood in the half-open screen door. His two hands cupped her cheeks again, and he kissed her fiercely. Her eyes were still closed when he said, "It's now, Tally. Now is right."

He was halfway down the steps before she recovered from this third kiss. "Pick you up about eleven tomorrow," he called jubilantly to her and anyone who might be listening. Joshua Dale Smith whistled all the way back to the street. She listened until the Jeep's motor obliterated the tune.

Jo Ellen Warbonnet Red Leggins did not whistle, nor hum, nor smile. She hissed. "What's got into you, Joshua Smith?" Christy looked sharply at the back door and back at her mother, hoping the two teenagers didn't hear.

"Something happened—to both of us—when I drove her home from the airport, Grandmother. There's no controlling this thing; you should know that." Jo Ellen's romance and subsequent elopement with the young Assiniboine whom her Sioux family didn't want her to marry was legend on the reservation.

"I'm going to take it real slow, Jo Ellen. Give her plenty of time to back out of it. But I just need to ask you two to speak well of it, or not at all, in front of the kids. Please?" He looked beseechingly at Christy, whose countenance was stern and still. Jo Ellen was holding her breath, biting her tongue, as he continued. "Okay, I knew I could count on you to do right by me. I'll talk to the kids at supper. Christy, I'd love to have you, but I think I'd better be alone with them this time, okay?"

She sniffed and walked into her bedroom.

James-Dale and Ellen climbed into the Jeep, both talking at once. "I've got almost six hundred dollars, Dad," the boy crowed. "What kind of a car can I get for that much money?"

"I made seventeen free throws in a row at the field today, Dad," Ellen Joy countered. "I'm trying to practice a little every day."

"Whoa, whoa!" Joshua was overjoyed at their babbling. "One at a time, please. Isn't it early to think of a car, James-Dale? By the time you finish driver's education next year, you'll be sixteen. And have a lot more money saved, I expect! Can't get much for six hundred bucks, but it's sure a good start." He turned to his daughter. "I'm going to make it a point to get to every home game next year, Ellen. Maybe some out of town ones, too. Now, I'm heading for the rib joint again. Is that right?"

Brother and sister were still gnawing at rib bones when he broached his subject. Grandfathers, he'd asked, please protect my children from my passions and from the world.

"I'm seeing a woman—dating a woman—now, kids. She's Tally Carver, the new Controller at the Tribal office. I wanted to tell you before you heard it somewhere else." He sat and watched them take in this information, chew their mouthfuls of ribs and beans, and swallow.

"'Bout time, Dad. Go for it!" Ellen Joy was guileless. She was happy if Joshua was happy.

"She's a white woman, isn't she, Dad?" James-Dale was frowning, running his fingers under his beaded headband and tossing his black Indian hair. "Drives a little Oldsmobile?"

"Yes, she is. She's from Virginia, but doesn't have much of a southern accent at all. Attraction or love, my children, doesn't see race or creed. It just feels the other person's heart.

You'll know that soon, yourself, and won't want to be too quick to judge today."

James-Dale pushed on. "Are you marrying her, or what?" His jaw jutted out at Joshua now, and he was determined to outstare his father.

Joshua's reply was stern, but still couched in the same loving vein in which he began the conversation. "We just spent most of today together, and the ride from the airport a week ago Wednesday. It's too soon to think of marrying, my *chos-kay*, and I am not going into 'or what' with you. But I am certain I am in love with her. Surely, if she felt the same way, we'd marry."

He finished his talk, addressing them both. "This will give you time to get used to the idea. I know you will have the respect for my feelings that your aunt and grandmother have taught you all these years. Talk it over when you're alone and let me know when you feel like meeting her."

They knew the discussion was over. There was forced conversation on the way home. James-Dale would help his father clear the weed field at the Valu-Wear apartment building on Tuesday. Yes, Ellen could help at $5.00 per hour. Was there a soft drink in Dad's cooler? The ribs made you so thirsty. The ride finally ended. His daughter hugged him goodnight. James-Dale, skirting the edge of familial respect, hung his head and waggled his hand.

Jo Ellen's porch light was on, and Christy stepped out and down the front steps. "Need to talk to your dad for a minute," she told her niece and nephew as they passed her. "Check the puppy's food and water, will you two?"

She stood at the bottom of the painted porch steps, illuminated in the light that battled the burgeoning dusk. The black halo of her hair encircled her lovely oval face. Her big, deepest brown eyes were not flashing at him now, but were filled with the love and respect he'd recently come to know from his sister-in-law. "Okay if I get in the Jeep for a minute, Joshua Dale?" She was tentative, afraid of what she wanted to discuss.

"Well, yeah, Miss Christmas! Nothing changes because my fool heart has gone a-tumbling, surely." He decided on this approach with Christy as she paused at the steps. *I am probably in love; she will always be the beloved sister-in-law and aunt.* "C'mon, we'll go get a bottle of pop."

He headed downtown, where the Mini-Mart would still be open. "Good dinner?" *Christy was going to have a hard time getting to the point.*

"Yup. Same old wonderful ribs. That James-Dale can eat his weight in them. I'll take you and Grandma next time." He pulled in to the combination service station and late-night convenience store and excused himself to go inside and buy sodas.

"Here you go, ma'am, ice cold Pepsi One, just like you like it!" He handed her the can and got back behind the wheel, sipping thoughtfully on lemon tea. "What's on your mind, Christy? Spit it out. Your input is important to me, you know."

"Okay, Joshua, here goes." Christy was anxious now, and her words raced. "Forget that she's white; forget that you've only known her sixteen minutes. You said about Mom and Dad, and I know it's true about not being able to pick the spots where love lights." She paused, out of breath, and took a drink. "But, Joshua, Mom will go berserk if you take the kids away from us. Not to mention James-Dale will have a lot of trouble with a white stepmother, anyway. I can tell that look on Mom's face; she'll go to the Council or something. Oh, Joshua, they've been with us all their lives!" A fat trail of tears streaked both her toasted-almond cheeks.

"Here, here, Sister," Joshua patted her jeans-clad thigh as he eased the Jeep to a halt on the street east of her house. He reached over and held her close. "Christy, honey, use your good head. Look here at me, now. Stop crying and think."

She sniffled and clung to him.

"Christy, I will never take the kids from your house, unless they ask to go. And, even then, it would have to be for love of me, not because they were upset at some goings-on with you or their grandmother. So don't worry about it. Not one bit. Also, you're pretty quick on the trigger, getting James-Dale a white stepmother! I'll admit, I believe myself to be in love with Tally Carver, but it's a long river ride from there to marriage. I intend to take it so slow that she has plenty of time to bow out gracefully." He paused, then went on, thoughtfully. "If we did marry, Christy, for the sake of argument, I would still not ask the kids to live with me. Their stability and happiness are more important to me than moving in on them and trying to be a full-time father after all these years. Surely, you can see how I have tried not to interfere with their home life in the three years I've been back?"

Christy was boo-hooing again. "Oh, Joshua, of course. I know you wouldn't. I don't know what I was thinking. I just—oh, Joshua—"

He held her again as he would a child, and let her weep for her own, unspoken loss.

Neither of them noticed the two-toned Cutlass as it passed on its way to the Mini-Mart. Tally could not believe her eyes. It was just four hours since Joshua had left her. She bought her orange juice and resolutely took an unfamiliar route home. In her kitchen, she bit her lip and did not weep. I have no shoulder to cry on, she thought.

Chapter Seven

He knocked at her door at five 'til eleven. She was finishing a fourth e-mail to her mother and friends back East. "Be right there!" she yelled down the hallway, not caring if he heard. She punched the 'Send' button, stood, stretched, and went to let Joshua in.

Her sweat pants and ribbon-tied hair were his first clue, but he hesitantly gave her the benefit of the doubt. "Not ready yet, Tally? I'll just grab a cup of—"

"I can't go, Joshua. I'm…um…not feeling well, and it's—I'm just not feeling well."

She's a poor liar, Grandfathers. Not good at it at all. His soothing, carefree reply belied a troubled heart. "That's okay, Tally. Can I have a cup before I go on to my grandfather's?" He moved toward the little half-full pot, its red light and the kitchen essence indicating that hot coffee was there, and waited for her assent.

"Okay, I guess. No, I don't want any." She sat in her recliner in the living room, legs drawn up, hugging herself. Joshua went to the couch, sat, and took careful sips of hot coffee. Silence reigned.

She's depressed. Beautiful. Looks like a mermaid on a rock, all drawn up like that. Will she tell me what's happened?

She didn't. "Well, I'm trying to catch up on my e-mail correspondence, Joshua," she hinted, making a motion as if to stand and leave the room.

He took a risk. "Tally Jo Carver, were you just playing with me yesterday?"

"Me? *Me!!*" she sputtered, and went silent again.

"I don't know what that means, dear one," he began, and was touched to see her demeanor soften at the endearment. "But if yesterday's people weren't playing games, they should be able to tell one another anything. Anything. Something has happened to make you sad or depressed. It happens, Tally, and it's okay that you don't want to go this time. But... those two people would tell each other. Yesterday, at least, they would have talked."

She was determined not to cry. "I was...disappointed... last night...to see you holding another woman. In your Jeep. Down by the Mini-Mart." The words came from her painfully, but without rancor. Then she babbled to cover up the feelings so noticeable in her tone. "I know it's none of my business...I don't have any reason to think...there's no reason why you shouldn't...you can do—"

He stepped across her low coffee table and put the flat of his hand against her still-murmuring mouth. "Buh...buh... buh..." it continued to gurgle.

"Hush now, Tally. Hush." He stood that way until she was silent. When he removed his hand, she walked away from his touch, to lean on the wall at the kitchen ell. She stood there and faced him defiantly until he spoke again.

"I want to say I expected different from you, Tally. But that's not fair. We don't yet know what to expect from one another. But yesterday's people would have faith beyond the grave. I will trust you with my living, beating heart. And I expect you to ask for an explanation, at least, before you get disappointed and sad at anything I may do." Joshua sighed at the end of his long speech and slumped into the chair she had vacated. He patted its arm lovingly, as if she still sat there.

"Oh, Joshua!" Tally was determined not to cry in front of him again. "Joshua, I wasn't wrong, was I? There *was* something between us yesterday. Something that would make it impossible for you to be with another woman just a few hours later. There *was* something, wasn't there?"

"Tally, darlin', what did I just take half a lifetime to put into words? Seems like the last thing we ever agreed on was that we were 'going together!'" They each chuckled cautiously at the thought.

Still smiling, Joshua went on. "Now, what that means to me is this: If I catch the shoe man hugging you like I was hugging my sister-in-law, I will first find out if you have something in your eye or just got some really bad news or something." He was nearly done with his comical pronouncement. "Then, and only then, will I kill him!"

That broke them both up. Uproarious laughter filled Tally's apartment and lightened their hearts.

She changed quickly, and they were down in the Jeep in fifteen minutes. Montana's huge sun warmed them as they drove slowly to the residential area on the other side of Poplar. Joshua waved at several people in their yards, all of whom returned his greeting.

"Nobody on the ground waved at me, Joshua, and I felt foolish." Tally's statement was a question.

"They didn't know you yet, Tally. They'll wave in their cars. When you are driving, it's like, 'Hello there, please drive carefully and save me and mine from harm.' On the ground it's 'Hello, my friend whose name I know!'" He turned a sharp corner with the Jeep and headed back a block, turned another corner. A round Indian woman in bib overalls was on her knees in a flowerbed on Tally's side of the road.

"There's Blue Cloud, working in the yard she's so proud of. Wave a 'hello,' Tally." His broad smile was proprietary as his woman received a smile and a flourish of gardening tool in return.

Raymond Wooden Headress's home was a square, white, two-bedroom tribal house. It differed from its neighbors by an open, atrium entrance to a huge, all-weather screened porch. They parked on the street in front of the neat yard.

From the small paper sack on the front seat between them, Joshua took a flat, brown can. "Tobacco for my elder," he indicated to her matter-of-factly. They walked the path to the porch shoulder-to-shoulder, not touching.

"Grandfather, you there?" Joshua peered to the left into the darkened interior of the porch.

"Come in, come in! Who's that with you?"

Joshua opened the door, entered, and held it for Tally. She stood in the doorway as he approached his grandfather, placed the Copenhagen in the blanketed lap, and shook hands with the old man.

"Grandfather Raymond Wooden Headdress, I've brought Tally Carver to lunch with us. Tally, my grandfather."

He looked like everyone's image of a medicine man, if you discounted the white shirt and brown bolo tie with its large agate decoration at his corded neck. And the leather, slip-on house shoes on his feet, she thought. Not to mention that big revolver in the leather holster hanging on the side of his chair. His gray hair was in a single braid. The square face it framed was a road map of the reservation, its deep-set black eyes inquisitive and alert. She could not believe he was ninety-three years old, and she didn't know what to do next.

"I'm so proud to meet you, sir," she began.

He held out a huge, veined hand, and his voice was soft, rusty. "Welcome to my home, child. Welcome. Let's see what Dora has for lunch. Dora!"

An immense woman of indeterminate age appeared at the home's open front door. "I'm right here, Raymond," she groused. "No need to yell."

"Miss Tally Carver here will help you get the lunch on. Tally, this is Dora Moses. She's a Sioux. Ancient mortal enemy. Heh, heh!"

Tally followed Dora's waddle into the large kitchen.

It was hard to be uncomfortable in the woman's kitchen. It was spotless, gleaming with white appliances, and smelled of something wondrous bubbling on the electric range. In the room's exact center sat an island of well-used black and chrome wood stove. Some living greenery and copper-bottomed pots decorated its top and two padded maple chairs sat by each side.

"It's a marvelous old stove," Tally said. Dora was silent, stirring the pot. "What can I do?"

"The men just wanted to be alone. Tobacco, you know. I 'spect Joshua needs some advice about you. You two serious?" Dora put the cover back on the luncheon soup and fixed Tally with her gaze. "Huh?"

"Should I call you Dora?" Tally spoke with respect to the nosy old woman. When Dora nodded and continued her unbroken gaze, Tally went on.

"Really, Dora, we just met. I've only been here ten days. I'm the controller—" Dora interrupted.

"I know who you are, Tally. This is a small reservation. Everybody knows who you are. Everybody knows who Mr. Marsden is. And everyone—every single person on this reservation—knows and loves Joshua Smith. So...are you serious or not?"

Tally capitulated. "Oh, Dora, I'm head-over-heels. What am I going to do?" Her dark, blue-gray eyes entreated the older woman.

A brief, wide smile transformed Dora's round, brown face. "Have lunch with his grandfather, I think. Go in there and set another place from the china cupboard, girl. It will be fine."

Lunch was a thick soup, broth with garbanzo beans and unrecognizable, delicious ingredients. It came to the table in shallow Limoges soup bowls, delicate spheres of eggshell with teal and coral flower splashes. A loaf of homemade wheat bread sat on a board in the table's center, a basket of piping hot corn muffins and a glass-and-silver bowl of chokecherry jelly near the old man's hand at the head of the table. Ornate, heavy sterling flatware graced each place. Raymond's hogleg now hung in its holster at the side of his antique dining room chair.

Tally and Joshua sat on one side of the lace-covered table, and Dora seated herself opposite them. "Grace, Raymond?" Dora's reminder was not necessary. Raymond's arms were outstretched.

"Great Spirit of my grandfathers, ruler of my earth, God of all things. We thank you for the fruit of your blessing, our children, and this food. O-ho!"

"O-ho!" Joshua breathed, as Dora crossed herself, and Tally said a soft amen. "Let's eat this Mexican stuff!"

"Tally," Raymond began, when breads and muffins were buttered, condiments passed, and the menudo in the soup plates was cooling. "Tally, did Dora tell you about Mama's cook stove?"

Dora was shaking her head vigorously.

"Well, Mama and me retired from the ranch about twelve years ago. That was the last year I roped for branding. Mama said no one but an old fool would be out there roping after he was eighty. They built this house 'specially for us. Everyone said, 'Mama, what a treat you're going to have...a new modern kitchen, everything at your fingertips.'"

Joshua was beaming at his grandfather and casually hugged Tally's neck. Chills were visible down Tally's side at his caress. Dora regarded them beatifically. Raymond continued his tale.

"The second day she stopped cooking. She wouldn't make me another blessed thing until I got them to haul in the old wood stove from the ranch and put a hole in the ceiling for the stovepipe. Dora here had to sneak me food to keep me alive!" He laughed softly and retreated into the memory of his dead wife, who cooked and baked his favorite things on a wood stove into the 1990's.

Huckleberry pie and ice cream finished the meal. Tally had to ask about the delicious, tart fruit in the dessert. "I'm afraid I didn't know there really were huckleberries," she laughed to all. "Except in Tom Sawyer stories, I mean."

Joshua told her she'd appreciate the pie a lot more after he took her huckleberry picking in August. "A *lot* more," he reiterated. "Won't she, Grandfather?"

"You just come on over here, child," Raymond chided his grandson. "I buy 'em off Indians who come around to sell them. Dora puts them in the freezer here and at her place. You don't have to grub for them if you don't want to, and don't let this fool kid tell you different!" His love for Joshua was so apparent, the room was filled with it. The grandfather caught Tally's eye, and his leathery wink delighted her. "You women clear this table, now, and the boy and I will tell lies and talk business."

They washed and dried the Limoges and the sterling by hand in comfortable silence. Dora piled the rest of the dirty dishes into the dishwasher. "Come out back, I'll show you Raymond's outdoor flowers." She walked Tally to the back door, and they spent half an hour away from the house, Dora's obvious reason for the garden excursion.

Raymond was back in his chair on the porch, Joshua on the floor in front of him, when Tally came back to the house. "'Bout ready to go, Tally?" He stood and made departing noises.

"Dora, get Mama's box," Raymond called. She came immediately and placed in his lap a large trinket box covered with seashells. He opened the hinged lid and looked at the contents with indescribable devotion. After a moment, he chose something and closed the lid.

"Thank you for coming to my home. Thank you for the smile on my grandson's face and the lightness of his step." He was serious, reverent, as he handed her the brooch.

It was a delicate fleur-de-lis, three golden stalks topped with shiny black daisy petals. Each daisy's center was a half-carat diamond. She held it in her outstretched palm, raising her eyes to Joshua, who had moved slightly to the rear of his grandfather. He was nodding his head firmly at her, and she could not refuse the gift.

"I am so honored, Grandfather Raymond," she began, and could speak no more. Silent tears spilled from her eyes, were salty rivers on her cheeks.

Joshua and his grandfather shrugged their shoulders at each other. *Women!* Their gesture was clear. Tally brushed at her face with her left hand, and held the brooch to her lips. "It's my second Montana treasure," she told the old man simply. "Thank you."

They expressed their regards to Dora for the meal and made their retreat from the porch and back to the Jeep. "Where to now, ma'am?" Joshua was jovial.

"How about the towns of Scobey and Flaxville, up and back, just so I know what they're about?" Tally was wrapping the brooch in paper towel from his floorboard and placing it gently in her purse. He pointed the Jeep toward the highway.

"What was your first?" He spoke much later, as they approached the turnoff at Wolf Point.

"First? Beg pardon, what first do you mean?" Now she was confused. Did he want to know about her sexual experience?

"Treasure, darlin', don't look so alarmed. Grandma's brooch is your *second*, you said."

"Oh, Joshua, pull over here a minute. Yes, that's good." She scooted over to him and turned up her face for a kiss.

"That's better," she sighed contentedly when they knew each other's lips for all time. "A 'going-together' girl shouldn't have to wait until mid-afternoon for a kiss, should she?" Sliding back to her seat, she punched his shoulder playfully. "Should she?"

He started up the engine, not willing to repeat his original question.

She hesitated a moment, then told him the simple truth. "It was the sweet grass, beloved. The sweet grass you burned, and the braid that you gave me. My first Montana treasure."

He was visibly touched, both by her endearment and by her confession. He offered the explanation his pride had prevented him from giving her this morning. "Christy and Jo Ellen were afraid I was going to take the kids from their home, Tally. She was crying."

Tally felt no need to talk of it again and leaned her head back to let the Jeep's natural air-conditioning cross her neck and shoulders. "I want to know so many things, Joshua. You just stop me if I shouldn't ask, okay? Like, on a need-to-know basis?"

He spoke above the wind noise of the highway and the rattling of the Jeep. "Nothing I won't tell you, Tally, if you feel you have to ask. But I should tell you right now…no, I have to stop again…" He pulled over on the shoulder.

Dead serious and without touching her, he spoke. "I intend to take this real slow, Tally. Real, *real* slow. These sweet kisses could carry us away, give us a burnout love affair. Then leave either or both of us thinking we owe the other something. It's possible that I have been waiting for you to come by my window for all of my life. Surely, I can spare a few more weeks or so."

He had described her relationship and marriage to a "T". A burnout love affair, nose-diving into misplaced loyalty. How wise was her man, this Joshua Dale Smith. She was content. "Okay, Joshua. You lead." She patted her purse. "I'll just accumulate treasure."

Flaxville and Scobey were just more of the same flat, brown Montana scene. They had hot dogs and root beer floats at a picnic table at Scobey's Dairy Queen. A gaggle of brown and white children ran, squealed, and dropped their cones indiscriminately. "Dairy Queens are the same, no matter where you are," she observed.

He was quiet, watching and eating, wondering if his two had ever dropped cones at Dairy Queen.

Her curiosity overcame her while they were driving home. "There's a sketch on the dining room wall, Joshua. Your grandfather's dining room. It's pencil on white paper in a little black frame. I've seen the painting. 'Roping the Bear,' or something like that. Charles Russell. Joshua, that sketch is signed C. Russell. Is it—could it be real?"

He chuckled. "Have Grandpa Raymond tell you about Charlie Russell next time we visit, Tally. He was on the ranch when Grandpa was a boy. Great-grandpa Iron Man Wooden Headdress said Charlie saw them rope that bear right out there by Square Butte, and sketched it immediately. Raymond says that Gray Cow, my great-grandma, liked the sketch so much she bedeviled Charlie in Assiniboine until he drew another one and gave it to her. They found it when she died, years later, in the big elk hide bag she kept by her pallet."

Tally was nodding, still perplexed. "And there's some logical reason for Louis XV furniture that looks real, Limoges china, and sterling knives that weigh a pound apiece, I guess?"

He was playfully stern. "Do you think other cultures don't love beautiful things, too, Miz Carver? No, scratch that! That sounded critical, and I don't want to discourage your curiosity. Let me start over again."

His delivery was theatrical. "Yes. There is a logical explanation. Oil. Money doesn't mean a thing to Grandpa Raymond, but he bought Grandma anything and everything she ever asked for. She loved a beautiful table setting. And France. She loved France."

"Oh." She was silent until they were within sight of her apartment building, not brave enough to ask about France today. At her door, she tried to keep him longer. "Shall we watch some television, Joshua? Or put in a movie? I have some good ones."

He hugged her briefly and stepped back. "You know, darlin', I went without TV for so many years, I learned to get along without it. A movie might be good, some other time. This afternoon I have to go home, get ready for a big week." He saw her disappointment.

"Tell you what. Do you have the last explode-'em-up Bruce Willis movie? *Die Hard For the Last Time*, or whatever it is? My kids wanted to see it when it was in Glasgow, and I guess it's out on video now. We'll be clearing this weed field here on Tuesday." He looked out at it with an expert eye. "Looks like about three hours for the three of us. I'll start 'em out about two in the afternoon. Maybe you'd offer us a cold drink when you get home from work? And then a movie here and take-out hamburgers might be in order?" Forgive the scheme, Grandfathers. But I know they will love her, too.

Tally brightened at the prospect of Joshua on Tuesday. It would only be later, as she called Bob Wilson and asked him to rent the video in Glasgow for her, that she began to dread the first confrontation with his teenagers. Right now, she was cheerful.

"Wonderful! We'll do that. See you then." She turned to go into her apartment, and stopped for one more question.

"Joshua, I guess I don't understand this gift thing. Rosie gave me something, and also gave you something. Your grandfather made me such a wonderful present. Why didn't he give you anything?"

He was starting down the stairs. His rugged face was gleeful as he turned it up to her one final time. "What makes you think he didn't?"

He whistled all the way to the street.

Chapter Eight

monday passed quickly, with Tally and Bob and Sarah Grey Wolf involved in finalizing the Accounts Payable analyses they'd been separately working on for days.

"Bob, will you stay a minute?" Tally said. It was after five and the accounting office was empty. "I need some clarification here."

He explained the Miscellaneous Expenditure of $12,000 to date. "That's two thousand a month to Mr. Marsden, the manager of the shoe factory. It's a consulting expense, really, we should probably charge it to—"

Tally interrupted him. "What does he consult, Bob? Whom does he consult? What's it for?"

"You know, Tally, I really and truly don't know. It's Ezra's deal. You'll have to ask him. I just know we have an annual expenditure form, signed by Ezra, authorizing this monthly disbursal. I do, however, think not everyone in the world knows about it. So you'd better ask Ezra personally, okay?"

Ezra would return from a routine trip to Washington, D.C. on Friday morning. She made a notation on her desk calendar and remembered to thank Bob again for bringing her the rental movie as they left the Tribal offices together.

She dressed down on Tuesday, in good pressed jeans and a seersucker blazer, because she didn't want to look overdressed to Joshua's teenagers. She felt practically useless as she commanded the accounting troops that day and finally left early, asking Bob to lock up for her. There were cold drinks in the refrigerator in her apartment. She had popcorn for the microwave, and trepidation in her heart.

Am I doomed if they don't like me? Should I have asked? Oh, God, I haven't been a teenager for a hundred years! Her thoughts were chaotic as she pulled into her parking space at 4:30.

The weed field was partially visible as she got out of the car. An Indian teenager—James-Dale, she supposed—was driving a little garden tractor with a rake attached. She took the long way around the building to pass the three workers in the fenced field. She called out, "Hi!" and waved cheerfully to Joshua, who came toward her immediately. A pretty teenager followed in his wake.

She smiled at the girl. "Hot out here, isn't it? Could you guys use a cold drink?" Tally wasn't good at subterfuge, but Ellen Joy didn't seem to notice.

They spoke at the same time, Joshua making introductions and Ellen overriding him with, "Yes, please! Dad's cooler's been empty half the afternoon. And he's such a slave driver!"

"Ms. Carver, my thirsty daughter, Ellen Joy Smith. Ellen, this is Tally Carver." He waved his arm round and round at the boy on the rake. "We're nearly done here, Tally. Why don't we come up and get a drink when we're finished?"

Ellen's face fell, and Tally made a quick decision. "I'll bring you a can of something down, Joshua. Then you guys can come up afterwards, if you want to, okay?" Joshua looked puzzled even as the girl's face brightened. "Pepsi or 7-up for you and your brother, Ellen?"

Ellen chose, and Tally brought three cold cans to the fence gate and did not linger. The girl thanked her exuberantly and skipped into the field to take a drink to her brother. Joshua looked at his can of lemon tea thoughtfully. He watched her retreating back with eyes of love before turning to rejoin his children. Okay, Grandfathers, it's *really* up to you now.

The knock came at five-thirty. Tally was overjoyed, for by this time she was sure they'd finished and left. A smiling Joshua stood there, flanked by a happy girl and sullen boy. "Fill 'em up, ma'am?" Father and daughter laughed as they held out their empty cans. The three trooped in, brushing themselves off on the walkway before entering her kitchen.

"Help yourselves there in the fridge, guys. I'm just try-ing to decide what to use for a coffee table book. Maybe you can help me? This book of antique maps, or this shooting script of *Wolf Dancer*?" A look of interest appeared on James-Dale's face in spite of himself. He was 'into' acting, Joshua had said.

Ellen spoke. "The book is pretty. The other is kind of… scruffy."

"Yeah, I know you're right. I just love the script so much, signature and all." She nodded her head toward the director-star's bold, black autograph, placed the maps on the coffee table and laid the script carelessly on the kitchen counter.

"Won't you guys come in and sit? It's my popcorn supper night. I make popcorn and watch a movie. I've got the latest Bruce Willis, my secret passion!" Why am I babbling? she thought. I've done enough. It's in the lap of the gods now.

"I've wanted to see that flick, Tally," Joshua began. "But only if we can bring you some burgers and onion rings to go with your popcorn." Swept along by the adults' charade, Ellen seated herself in the living room with Tally while James-Dale and his dad went to get burgers.

Tally began with the usual innocuous questions about school and hobbies. Ellen answered politely, all the time eyeing the combination TV/VCR. She quizzed Tally at her first opportunity to speak. "Is the movie in already?" She stepped to the screen when Tally replied in the affirmative.

Ellen Joy turned and looked into Tally's soul.

She must resemble her dead mother, Tally thought, but that look is pure Joshua.

"I think this is real important to my dad," Ellen said. "I don't think James-Dale will stay, unless maybe we're into the movie when he gets back."

Tally was impressed. "Okay, we'll move it ahead, and you can be in charge of the clicker—the remote control—does that work for you?"

Ellen was already expertly fast-forwarding the movie past the previews, so her hostess guessed that it worked for Ellen Joy Smith. Their unspoken conspiracy began.

Opening credits were rolling over exploding radar scanner towers when Joshua and James-Dale opened the door. The many sacks they carried emitted tantalizing odors. According to plan, the sound of the movie brought James-Dale to the kitchen ell, where Tally had leaned in confrontation with his father just a few days before.

"Did you watch any, Ellen?" The boy nonchalantly eased himself into the living room, toward the sofa and his sister. "Did anything happen before this?" It was obvious he was hooked, and Tally breathed a sigh of relief and went to help the senior Smith with the bags.

She was rummaging in the bottom cupboard for paper plates when he spoke loudly, for the benefit of the children. He made silent kissing gestures at her in order to make sure she understood his ulterior motive.

"I'll look at that closet door for you before I forget it. Which room is it?" She smiled knowingly and preceded him into the hallway. There she stood in her bedroom doorway and flung herself against the doorjamb, a happy grin on her face. Her provocative stance was wasted on Joshua. He reached her in two giant steps and enfolded her in his arms before she even had her pose perfected.

Working man's sweat stung her nostrils, not unpleasant as it overlaid sweet grass and melded with the fragrance of the hand soap in her bathroom. The long, hard kiss asked more than any previous had done, and she moved in to him without hesitation. Oh, my God, we fit perfectly! She was glorying in that fit as he stepped back a pace and bent to whisper in her ear.

"Cut it out! One of us has to remember we're taking it slow!" He hugged her shoulders, and they walked back to the kitchen. Ellen Joy watched them peripherally, and they did not fool her. The boy was deliberately engrossed in the movie.

The adults busied themselves in the kitchen. He patted her hand occasionally and made little faces at her, speaking the universal language of falling in love.

"Come and get this stuff!" Joshua held two plates in the direction of the living room so the teenagers wouldn't have to miss a beat of their movie. Tally put the two others on the kitchen table.

"C'mon, Dad, this is a great movie!" James-Dale tried to lure his father to the living room as he took the plate of burgers from him.

"I'll eat out here, first, *chos-kay,* where there's more room. Then we'll pick it up. The sound is sufficient right now. We won't miss much."

The boy shrugged in the manner of his father and went back to his seat on the couch.

They ate burgers and onion rings and drank lemon tea in silence. Joshua leaned across the table and twinkled at her. "It's our first meal at home, dear. Not bad, not bad. Can you cook anything else?"

"My pizza is great. Well, I don't know yet how great it is in Poplar, Montana. If you're after me for my cooking, you'll want to buy a cookbook—or go chase Dora instead."

He decided to tease her some more. "Well, be sure you get the recipe for that tripe soup from Dora. I could eat that stuff every meal." He watched slyly for a change of expression on her face. Tripe wasn't to everyone's taste, and he was sure she had not known the base stock of the Sunday soup. Tally was purposely angelic and wouldn't give him the satisfaction.

Finished with burgers, they took their two kitchen chairs into the darkened living room and gave themselves a good view of the last portion of the movie. He leaned to her again. "Aren't we supposed to 'neck' or something in the movies?"

"No, silly," she whispered back, giggling and causing Ellen to look up. "'Going together' people may only neck in movie theaters that seat seven or more. New Montana law!"

She'd grown to love that shrug, and he didn't disappoint her. Win some, lose some, it said. So he didn't even hold her hand, and they watched the exciting, mediocre story in relative silence. She served more cold cans without asking, and all turned down her popcorn gestures. At 8:15, the final credits rolled, and the boy and girl stood and stretched. Tally drew the drapes to let in the evening's sunset and excused herself to go to the bathroom.

She was silently jubilant when she returned. James-Dale was oh-so-casually looking at the script she'd left on the corner of the counter. She eased into conversation about the famous actor/director. "He spent a lot of time at the Bureau of Indian Affairs where I worked, before and during the first part of making the film. I did him a particular favor, and he even said I could be an extra in a fort scene if I wanted to. But I asked for this, and he said to remember he still 'owed me one' when he sent it." She put it in his hands, casually, as she spoke.

"This is the actual words from the movie, isn't it?" James-Dale held the script with awe as he spoke. He cut himself off abruptly. He had communicated with the enemy, and he knew it would be hard to resume his silent scorn.

Tally pretended not to notice. "Pretty much, I think, since it's the shooting script." She didn't want him to reject her, so was afraid to offer it. "Maybe sometime when you're not working every day, you might want to borrow it to read? Just let me know."

Raised well and always polite, James-Dale hung his head. "Thanks."

"Thanks for the movie and stuff, Tally." Ellen was exuberant as the Smiths headed for the door. Both teens waited for their father to exit first. He looked at Tally, then back at his children, shrugged and grinned.

"I know it's still daylight. But I think I will kiss my lady friend goodnight, anyway. You kids wanta watch?"

Brother and sister nearly fell over each other in a race for the door. Ellen's laughter was the peal of summer bells. When they were gone, he took both her hands.

"Such an afternoon. And you rented the movie. Thank you for buying me tea. I love you, you know."

His sweet kiss was so brief, she didn't have time to encircle him with her arms when his declaration hit a brain cell. "Be good, now," he admonished, as he hurried out the door and down the steps. His whistled tune had changed: "Happy Days Are Here Again."

"Well, sure, I'll be good, Mr. Smith!" Tally raged in mock anger at her kitchen walls. "What else? How long are we on the take-it-slow-and-easy plan, anyhow?" She knew she wasn't really serious. It was all so right. If the relationship was going to another level, it was obvious that her sweetheart would be the one to take it there. She leaned on the wall again at the corner of the kitchen, closed her eyes, and thought of the strength of him as he kissed her.

Went pretty well with the kids. Ellen is on my side—or at least she's on her dad's side. *Chos-kay* means first-born. I think I had better luck with the second-born today. She tidied the rooms as the movie rewound, and put it in her briefcase to give back to Bob Wilson on the morrow.

The workweek passed in a blur. Her neighbor, Candy, spoke to her twice when Tally saw her around the apartment, and a lady she passed on each morning's drive waved at her on Thursday. Tally waved back, exhilarated. She had received a 'ground wave' of her very own. Montana was growing on her, even if she didn't hear a word from Joshua.

He knocked on her door Thursday night at seven. "No, can't come in. Too dirty. Been helping a guy with a well."

He was, indeed, filthy. "Want to do something tomorrow night?"

"Well, sure, Joshua. Of course. What shall we do?"

"Dinner, dancing? Movie, burgers? Park at Fort Peck Lake? No, better scratch that one. My mama always told me to remember what kissin' leads to. What say we go eat at Wolf Point and see what there is to do around there the week before Red Bottom Days?" He flattened his face against the screen and gave her a pretend-kiss. "Miss me?" She didn't have time to reply before he was on the steps, yelling, "Wear that riding skirt, will you?" Then he was down on the street and starting up his flatbed.

Tally stared at the departing truck long after it disappeared down the highway. She was growing accustomed to the way of this taciturn man with his sly sense of humor, he who smelled of sweet grass and whistled very old tunes.

Ezra Bangs The Drum came to the office when he first returned to the reservation on Friday. He was pleased at the appearance of diligence happening in the outer office, and complimented Tally on her progress report, as well as her growing rapport with her accountant. As their brief meeting was concluding, she had one last question. "Why do we pay Gerald Marsden a $24,000 per annum 'consulting fee'?"

"Well, Tally, it's necessary. It's actually the cost of keeping the shoe factory here on the reservation. Valu-Wear's home office would move it in a New York minute if he didn't sway their vote, because it's not profitable and is so far away, and their plans for western expansion are on hold for now."

She nodded, still not convinced.

"It's much, much less expensive than the cost of taking care of the 212 people who work there, most of them with families, after they run out of unemployment. Trust me, it's cheap at half the price. But Tally, it's a well-kept secret. I can count on you, of course?"

She reassured him, and they finished their business before noon. Ezra went home to the wife he hadn't seen all week, and Ms. Tally Carver indulged herself in busywork all afternoon. Often, she sat with her chin in her hands, contemplating the varied possibilities of an evening in her divided skirt.

She was sitting in such a manner when the telephone on her desk rang. It caused her to jump and spill her pencil box. "T. J. Carver," she said.

"G. E. Marsden here, Tally! I'm calling from Hartford. I'll be at Billings airport by noon on Saturday. If I race straight to my car in long-term parking, don't pass Go or collect any money, I can be home by five. How about dinner tomorrow night?"

"Oh, Gerry, I can't. So much has happened. I'll tell you everything when you get here. Sunday, maybe. But I can't go to dinner."

He didn't press her. "I'm very disappointed, of course, but I'll look forward to seeing you when I can. Bye now, Tally."

After she hung up, she didn't resume her daydreaming. *How am I going to tell him I've practically committed myself to Joshua Smith? It sounds real stupid, even to me, and I'm involved in it.*

On the way home, she tried to put herself in a better frame of mind, psyching herself up for dinner with her sweetheart. *If telling Gerry is the worst thing that happens,* she thought, *this love affair will be a snap.*

She didn't know she had received an e-mail from her ex-husband as she consoled herself with that thought. Doug Holcomb's communiqué waited in the small bedroom she'd converted to her at-home office. She heard the computer tinkling at her as she hurried into the apartment to shower and dress for Joshua. "Tally Carver, you've got mail!"

Chapter Nine

I'll read my mail while my hair is drying, Tally decided, as she threw her briefcase on the bed and stripped off her clothes. The computer tinkled again as she stepped into the shower. It would nag her every five minutes until she either took the message off or disconnected its reminder feature.

She dusted her body lavishly with the palest of silky peach powders. The towel threatened to slip each time she bent her head. Dinner in Wolf Point. Wear my riding skirt. She checked her naked body in the bathroom's three-way mirror. Lost a little weight, I think. Short lunches and long, long nights. Oh, well, that is soon going to change, if I get any vote at all!

Covered with a short, lightweight robe, Tally padded to the little bedroom and printed her e-mail. There was a cheery note and cute joke from a friend at the B.I.A., some SPAM from the National Association of Accountants, and a cryptic declaration from her ex-husband.

Leaving now. You come back, I stay there, I don't care. I need you and will spend the rest of my life making it up to you. Your Doug.

Her gold Seiko said it was 7:45 in Maryland. She went to the phone, punched in the area code, and then stopped, momentarily elated. His phone numbers were in her day runner. How sweet it is! I've forgotten his number already.

There was no answer. "Call me before you do anything, Doug. I need some help from you." That worked with most people. Everyone liked to help someone else, or at least think they were doing so. "Here's my Montana number, and my work number, if you don't get this message until Monday." His answering machine beeped at her just as she finished reciting the second number.

Tally stubbed her bare toe on the recliner trying to replace the phone and do several beautifying things at once, and swore at the ceiling. "Damn! Damn, *damn*, DAMN!" There was no doubt in her mind that Doug Holcomb was on his way to Montana. She hoped he was driving.

She opened the door to Joshua at seven, her mind refreshed and determined not to think of any upcoming confrontation with her former husband. Joshua looked at her with approval and longing. The approval, she was sure, was for his grandmother's brooch pinned in the knot of her neck scarf. Longing was confirmed when he reached for her.

"I've smelled your hair since Tuesday, Tally. Awake, in my dreams, all the time. I had to pull out six fence posts today. The line was off about ten degrees. What am I going to do about you?"

She raised her lips to his. Again, she thought she'd weep at the emotion in his kiss. "Well, feed me, for starters!" She ran her index finger along a new, scabbed scratch on his left arm and looked at him quizzically.

"Yep. Getting careless, too. I may not live to enter into matrimony. Maybe not even into Wolf Point!" He squeezed her again and released her just as quickly. "C'mon, we're burnin' daylight!"

Matrimony? Now we've gone from "seeing each other" to "going together" to matrimony? He's thinking of marriage? Testing it on me? Could I marry him? She was solemn at his side. And, if not, why am I doing this?

A dinner crowd occupying the roadhouse near Wolf Point was fairly boisterous by the time they got there. "Should have started a little earlier on a payday night, I guess," he whispered to her, when they finally got a booth. "Are you okay with this? They make the best breaded prawns in the universe in this place, and I was hungry for them."

"Oh, Joshua. Prawns are my second favorite thing! I sure won't mind a little noise to have the best in the universe."

"No, nothing from the bar," she told the tired waitress. "Nothing for me, anyway. A cup of black coffee as quickly as you can, I think."

He opened his mouth as if to demur at the no-drink order, then thought better of it. They studied the menus, each busy checking out the entrees they were not going to order.

"Smith? Josh Smith? Well, looky here, guys!" A bow-legged, fortyish Indian stopped short as he passed their booth. A brown bottle of beer waved in his left hand. Many other beers were under his belt, Tally was sure. Two other men in the same wobbly condition soon joined him.

They had erupted from the open door of the barroom, a miasma of stale alcohol and cigarette smoke attending them. When all three were at the couple's side, the original fellow slid into the booth beside Tally. "How ya been, Joshua? Heard you was back on the rez."

"Johnny Painted Rock, this is Tally Carver. Over here, we have Junior Herbert and—well, one of the Goldshield boys." Joshua was polite and no-nonsense at the same time. The drunks all tried to shake hands at once.

"I'm senior now," Herbert moaned. "My old daddy died last year." Both he and the nameless Goldshield "boy" leaned on the high booth.

Johnny was careful not to touch Tally as he sat beside her, but his body odor caused her to slide surreptitiously away from him. "You buyin' a drink, Smith?" Johnny was not quite belligerent. "Workin', are ya?"

"I don't use it anymore, Johnny." Joshua was quiet and friendly, and she'd never before heard him use this tone of voice. "So I don't buy it anymore, either."

"Damn! Lot of that goin' around these days, old son!" Johnny Painted Rock stood and slapped the side of his disreputable Levis and laughed uproariously at his own wit. His two cronies chortled drunkenly and repeated the phrase as all three shuffled away, their voices fading into the background noise of people talking, silver and dishes clattering.

"Lot of that goin' around!"

Their waitress was a middle-aged white woman, sick of the Painted Rocks of the world, night after Montana night. She came to take their prawns order as soon as the inebriated trio had left their booth. She attempted to brighten up, as a nice tip was in order from the Indian man who'd want to impress his date. Her joviality was so forced, they were each grateful when she left them to reasonable silence.

"Lot of alcoholism on the rez, Tally. Lots more than the B.I.A. statistics will tell you. I was fortunate to beat it. I need to be an example of tolerance to those still in it. I hope you weren't too put off by those guys."

"I feel so safe with you, Joshua," she began, and he could not dismiss the look of love in her darkened eyes. "It wouldn't have bothered me even if they'd been rowdy, and they weren't. Just kind of...well...sad. They made me sad, anyway."

The jukebox was playing a Garth Brooks number. A couple was up on the six-foot dance floor across the room. "Would you like to dance, Tally?" Joshua watched her face carefully.

"Well, not really. But it would be an excuse to be close to you. I don't really care much for dancing."

How she loved to watch him when he really got tickled. Her man hee-hee-hee'd until tears came to his eyes. When he could squeak out a complete sentence he exclaimed, "Whew! What a relief. I was afraid that dancing was going to be your first favorite thing!"

The jukebox changed tunes, and the dancing couple left the floor and came in their direction. "It's my sister-in-law, Christy," he said to her. "That's Ezra's fourth or fifth son she's with. They go together once in a while." He waved in their direction.

Christy resisted the pull of young Bangs The Drum's arm, but the couple was nonetheless soon at their side. "Didn't expect to see you here, Miss Christy," Joshua sounded delighted. "Won't you sit with us for a minute? I want you to meet Tally."

Christy was wheedled into the booth, seated precariously on the edge of the seat at Joshua's side, still demurring. "We have a table on the other side, Joshua. We were just going to get some air."

"Anyway, Tally, this is my sister-in-law. The kids' aunt, Christy Red Leggins. And this is either Jerome or Nathan Bangs The Drum, right?" He smiled effortlessly at all, making the group a foursome for the moment.

"Nathan, I am," the solemn young man replied. "Pleased to meet you, Tally." He held out his hand. "I don't see much of my father, but he is raving about you every time I see him."

"Christy, this is the woman I told you and Jo Ellen about. Tally Jo Carver." He left it at that. Tally said a warm "Hello," as Christy sat resolutely, finally nodding in the white woman's direction.

"We gotta go, Joshua. Nice-to-have-met-you-Tally." Christy made her manners and left the booth. Her date followed in her wake, confused and muttering apologies.

As they demolished beer-battered prawns, Tally was playful. "That went well, don't you think, Joshua?" She giggled behind her napkin. "With the kids' aunt, I mean?"

He didn't think it was all that funny. "Part of the problems I said we'd encounter when we started seeing each other, Tally. Miss Christmas says she's worried about getting James-Dale a white stepmother. Could be the truth. But if we're for real, everyone will come around." He reached across and cupped her cheek in a way that made her squirm on the barely padded booth. "Don't weary your pretty head."

As they were leaving, Junior Herbert accosted them near the building, where it was dark from deepening sunset shadows. "Got a couple bucks? I'm outa gas."

"Sorry, pal, my date ate up everything I had on me," Joshua jollied his disheveled fellow tribesman, whose buddies were nowhere to be seen.

Junior stood with his hand out and did not even recognize them.

"Ah, ha!" Herbert bellowed drunkenly and slammed himself face first on the trunk of someone's car. "Lot of that going around these days!" He was still pounding and laughing when the Jeep left the parking lot, the arid gravel raising dust devils from the scuffling of his boots.

They drove west, away from Poplar, and Tally questioned their route.

"Thought I'd show you part of Fort Peck Lake while there was still a little light," Joshua mumbled around the restaurant's peppermint toothpick. "We'll go see the dam on a weekend day. You can't appreciate it at dusk. When they built it, it was the largest earth-filled dam in the world. Might still be, for all I know."

"Parking at Fort Peck Lake, Joshua?" Tally smiled slyly at him. "We've progressed from 'seeing each other' to 'Fort Peck parking' in the space of a week?"

He patted the top of her left thigh. "Nope. No parking." He fixed his eyes resolutely on the road, two hands on the wheel.

That was a perfectly reasonable, friendly caress, thought Tally. Nothing forward or lusty about it. Yet his touch makes my heart pound and my toes tingle. Surely, he senses this. Am I supposed to make the first move?

They drove about ten miles of the eighty-mile lake on the dammed Missouri before the growing dusk obscured her vision. "I'm going to head for the barn now, Tally. I have to work half a day tomorrow—stretching that fence that I didn't get done today because I was pulling out misaligned posts!"

It was too dark to see her face clearly, but he sensed its look of consternation. The Jeep was alone on the silent lake road as he came to a stop. An owl called.

Joshua held out his arms and she met him in the middle of the front seat. "Okay, honey. One little 'park,' okay?" He chuckled deep in his chest at his small joke and held her close and tight. She went limp and burrowed into his shoulder, drinking in the odor of sweet grass and reveling in his arms.

He was laughing again as their lips parted. Tally gasped for breath and railed at him. "What's so doggone funny? You're so serious all the time, and then you're laughing up a storm when you kiss me!" She was trying to keep a straight face.

"Oh, sweetheart!" Joshua was exuberant. "I've laughed more this week than I have in a dozen years. You heard my grandfather. He knows my heart is light because of you." He hugged her again. "No, I was just thinking about the first day I met you. I was so smitten I had to kick myself. I told myself then that I'd probably be offering Ezra many ponies for you before the week was out. Bride price, you know."

Not giggling now, she sat warm and content in his embrace. Bride price. Matrimony. I'm supposed to say something, I think.

"So, anyway, dear one, I was just wondering where I'd ever get ponies enough to pay the bride price for Tally Jo Carver!" He laughed again. "I wonder if old Ezra would take...ha, ha...installment ponies!"

She asked about James-Dale and Ellen as the Jeep retraced its route. The kids hadn't mentioned their evening at her apartment, he told her, and he indicated that no comment at all was probably the best indication of success. They talked about Bob Wilson and the tribal accounting office. She started to tell him of Gerry Marsden's monthly stipend and thought better of it. Confidentiality had no exemptions. They were soon at Tally's darkened apartment building. Far too soon to suit me, she thought.

"The couple next to you moved out mid-week," he said. "That apartment's empty. Candy must be up at Saco with her mama this weekend. Shoe man's still out of town. Does staying here alone bother you, Tally?"

"Not at all," she ventured quickly, and then wished she could bite off her tongue. He'd probably stay if I said I didn't want to be alone. As they reached her kitchen door, she chid-ed herself once again. No. No subterfuge. Joshua Dale Smith deserves better than the games of the world.

"Come in for just a little minute, Joshua. We'll split a can of your tea. There's something I have to tell you."

He held her at arm's length through the open door. His smooth, bronze face was nearly serious as he looked deep into her gray-green eyes in the kitchen's fluorescent light. "Miz Carver. You would not be tryin' to seduce me, would you?"

"Oh—you!" she spluttered and pretended to punch his chest as he crossed into her home and closed the door. "Get your own tea!" She wandered into the living room.

Joshua joined her, half the can of tea poured into one of her crystal glasses. He bowed and flourished the glass to her as she rejoiced that he made himself at home in her cup-boards. They spoke at the same time.

"Tally—"

"Joshua—"

"No, you go first," he said. Seated on the edge of her re-cliner, he sipped and watched her face.

"I told you I'd been divorced three years. But I didn't tell you that my ex-husband and I have been…close…occasion-ally during that time." She watched his face carefully for any sign that he didn't understand. A black look ripped across his countenance and was gone in a moment. He understood.

"Well, Joshua, I just got an e-mail. Sounds like he may have had too much to drink when he wrote it, but I tried to call him, and I'm very much afraid he's on his way here. To Montana. I wanted to tell you myself, in case he turns up." She heaved a great sigh, slumped, and drank some tea.

When he didn't respond, she tried again. "Well, that's it. What were you going to say?"

"Well, first I guess I have to say something else. *Ask* something else. Since I'm the new kid on your block. Any possibility of you and your former husband being…close…if he does come here?"

She was agitated, afraid he'd misunderstand. "No. Absolutely not. Doug Holcomb has two or three women at any given time. He just can't stand to let any of them go. He probably wants to lure me back into the Dougie-fold, but I was not interested even before I fell…I met you, Joshua."

His voice calmed her, and he remarked on her slip of the tongue without inflection. "I heard you the first time, sweet girl. Now, let me say what was on my mind, and then I really do have to be gone."

He tested the strength of the low coffee table and sat in front of her, holding both her hands. "I thought I'd make you dinner late afternoon tomorrow, Tally. At my place on the river. Rattlesnake or bear or something!" He chuckled at her grimace. "I don't want to rush you, girl. No obligation. But if you felt like spending the night, I wouldn't call the tribal police to send you home."

Whoopee! Going-together girls get fringe benefits! She tried to be as serious as he. "Okay, that's great. What time? Should I bring anything? Don't you take the kids for ribs on Saturday nights?"

"Come about four or so. Bring your jammies. Told them I'd take them Sunday night, and I was bringing my lady friend. Any other questions?"

"Yeah, I do have one. Why am I wearing the riding skirt?" She gestured at her outfit.

"Oh, that. Hard to get into, I figured. Not so tempting!" He rose to go while she still had a bewildered look on her face, because at a glance it was obvious he'd rather stay here with her.

Joshua adjusted the fit of his jeans without embarrassment. "Pajamas won't be a real necessity, Tally Jo Carver!" He bent over and kissed her mouth briefly. "Dream of me, my darlin', and come to me tomorrow. 'Night, now." He was out the door, admonishing her to throw the dead bolt, before she had crossed the living room.

Tally slow-danced to the door and locked it securely, imagining the scent of sweet grass as she leaned there. Her mind raced in slow motion. Jammies. Rattlesnake. Spend the night.

The harsh ring of the phone interrupted her reverie. She went to it and picked up the receiver with trembling hand, certain it was Doug Holcomb on the other end. She straightened her posture and assumed a business-like telephone voice. "Hello?"

"What's your first favorite thing?"

"Wha—what? Oh, Joshua, is that you? Where are you?" She relaxed in the recliner and caressed the side of her face with the phone.

"Stopped at the Texaco. You said prawns were your second favorite thing. What's your first?"

Tally placed a silent kiss in the business end of the receiver and giggled for the last time that evening. "Thought you'd never ask! I'll tell you tomorrow night!"

She whistled inexpertly on her way to the bedroom: "The Girl from Ipanema."

CHAPTER TEN

*T*ally *lay in a fragrant field of tall sweet grass. Below her bed in the small, trampled clearing rippled the river, lulling her senses. Rays from the overhead sun barely reached her body, so tall was the grass, but she was warm.*

The grasses rustled. Footfalls approached. He whistled "Thus Spake Zarathusthra." Languidly, she arranged her ankle-length apricot hair to showcase the daisy brooch and to make modest her nudity. She awaited the stranger's intrusion.

Bits of grass besmirched the empty half of the star quilt upon which she reclined, and she brushed at them, preparing him a place. The approaching rustle grew louder as she swept at the growing quantity of debris with her hands. Now the footfalls pounded, and each frantic swish at the quilt produced noisy jangles and tinkles. His shadowed copper face appeared above the sunswept grass. And faded…

"No, no!" Tally cried aloud as she fought to keep the dream. Her right hand began a rhythmic sweeping of the teal coverlet on her bed, and she surged back into half-sleep, but the pounding continued.

Soon she was fully awake, and not at all happy about it. As she slipped into her fuzzy robe, she realized that the phone had just ceased ringing, the computer was sending its obnoxious message again, and someone had been pounding on the kitchen door for a very long time.

Who could be at the door? I'll bet it's Joshua, on his way to work. Tally glanced at her watch. It's ten after nine! That's quite a sleep-in for me, and he is hard at work by now. She opened the door.

A scraggly Indian kid stood there, a disheveled white girl slightly to his rear. Neither one was more than seventeen or eighteen. "Mike here?" The boy rubbed his nose and hung his head. "Or Dottie?" She could barely hear this last question, aimed as it was at the wooden deck outside her kitchen door. The girl was silent.

She spoke to the beaded headband that encircled his black hair. "You must want the people who lived here before," Tally replied, covertly checking and grateful to see that the screen lock was in place. "I've just been here about two weeks."

The girl stamped her foot and muttered a curse. "You sure?"

The boy raised his head and challenged her answer. "No Mike? No Dottie? You can tell them it's Xavier Goes Along."

"Sorry, Xavier. Honest. It's my apartment now, and I have to get ready for company coming. Okay?" She made a motion as if to close the door, and Xavier Goes Along extended his grubby hands in supplication.

"You sure you don't know where they are?" he pleaded.

Tally shook her head. As she shut the door slowly on his hopeless face, she wondered what Joshua had meant. Exactly what kind of unsavory people had Mike and Dottie been? She listened at the door for many moments, until the sound of the young people's defeated footsteps reached the bottom of the outdoor stairs.

The bright Montana Saturday crept like a snail race. Tally tried to keep busy around her tidy apartment. The phone didn't ring again, and e-mail brought only cheery greetings from her mother.

The apartment building was still deserted. She had both washers and dryers all to herself in the first-floor laundry room. Between loads, she picked up accounting schedules she had spread on the spare bed, stared at them without comprehension, and laid them down again. Finally, she could stand the isolation no longer and grabbed her purse and car keys. A trip to the supermarket is in order, she thought. I need some groceries, and this early the stores won't be that crowded. Tally wasn't claustrophobic, but she was uncomfortable in close-packed crowds.

The essence of sweet grass was gone from her kitchen door area. Probably driven away by the aura of those strange kids. Wish I knew more about narcotics, she thought, I'd bet anything that boy was a doper. She retraced her steps across the living room to check the locks on the French doors. Finding them secure, she key-locked the kitchen dead bolt and skipped down the steps the sad young couple had descended just ninety minutes before.

She drove west, a steady 60 miles per hour on the highway. Her Cutlass ate up miles, and Tally loved to drive. Montana is surely the place for being alone on the highway, she thought. Today, she thought of Joshua as she drove, of his arms and his kiss and of their afternoon dinner today. If a thought of Doug Holcomb tried to intrude, she banished it immediately. I'll just cross that bridge when it gets here!

At Wolf Point, Tally looked at her watch. It was not yet noon, so she drove on toward Glasgow, where there were a few more shopping choices. She needed a wastebasket for the bedroom and a ream of laser paper, as well as laundry soap and fruit and many cans of lemon tea. The flat highway miles sped by. She flew through Frazer and Nashua, and soon she was entering the supermarket. I need to do routine chores today, she thought. Or I'll be giddy as a teenager by the time four o'clock comes.

Tally rounded the frozen food corner carefully. Her creaky shopping cart was half-full and wobbling. So much for routine, she told herself, as she took in the scene in the aisle. Christy Red Leggins and a short, wide, older woman were selecting ice cream. They were facing her, and she could not retreat.

"Christy! Hello. Nice to see you again." Tally was sincere. She wanted this gorgeous girl for an ally nearly as much as she wanted dinner and what might follow later in the day, on the banks of the Poplar River. When Christy did not immediately respond, she went on, "Is this your mother?"

Christy was sullen and silent. It was a helpless dichotomy, and her manners won out as she made introductions reluctantly. "Jo Ellen Red Leggins, this is Tally Carter. Joshua's friend, you know? Tally, my mother, the children's grandmother." Duty dismissed, the young Indian woman turned and began to examine the rest of the ice cream in the case, one carton at a time.

Tally held out her hand. Jo Ellen hesitated for a split second and touched it briefly. "It's Carver, Mrs. Red Leggins. Like woodcarver. Please call me Tally." She dropped her hand loosely at her side and locked gazes with Joshua's mother-in-law.

Jo Ellen's dark face was impassive. Deep-set eyes smoldered with curiosity and something else Tally didn't immediately recognize. Their heavily laden grocery cart partially obscured the woman's sturdy bulk. The sidelong glance she sent at her only living child said she knew there was no conversational help coming from that direction. Tally could tell that Jo Ellen didn't want to be cruel to her. She just didn't want to talk to the woman who was interfering in their life. Tally decided to save face for both herself and Joshua's family.

"So nice to meet you, Mrs. Red Leggins, and to see you again, Christy." Tally began preparing to take a hurried leave. As the words dropped from her mouth, three women came around the other end of the aisle and pushed two carts toward them. Jo Ellen was facing that direction. She elbowed her daughter and hurriedly began to speak in a loud voice.

"Glad the work is going well, Tally." Jo Ellen had a girlish smile. It belied the bulk of her body and caused its beholder to think of dancing slippers and sweet grass evenings. She was using the smile now, wafting it in the general direction of Tally and the oncoming trio. "You'll tell us all about it at the rib joint tomorrow night, eh?" She covertly elbowed Christy's haunch again.

"Oh, yeah. That'll be fun," Christy's reluctant two cents worth came into the conversation. Removing her face from the ice cream freezer and facing the oncoming women, Christy greeted them. "Hello, Mrs. Bangs The Drum. Hi, Eva. Hi there, Carlotta."

Ezra's wife was a dark brown woman of sixty-some years, short and with gray roots at the top of her black hair. She was dressed almost formally for her grocery outing in a crisp cotton suit of azure with a dated peplum and rolled collar. Nylon stockings covered her bony legs as far up as the world could see, and fashionable arch supporting shoes of a matching blue completed her ensemble. She waited for Jo Ellen to acknowledge her.

"Caroline, how nice to see you. It's been too long. You look lovely, as usual." Tally was certain Jo Ellen's tongue was in her cheek, but her attitude toward the Tribal Chairman's wife was warm and respectful.

Jo Ellen went on, enveloping Tally in the conversation. "You've met Tally Carver, of course? We were just talking about the kids and havin' a meal together and such. Oh, you haven't?"

She danced away from her grocery cart and somehow ensnared Christy and Tally, each on a short, round arm. They towered over her with tiny surrendered smiles on their faces, feeble pawns in Jo Ellen's charade as she introduced the First Lady of the sovereign nation of Fort Peck to the Tribe's new controller.

The unholy alliance severed the moment the Bangs The Drum group was out of sight. Christy escaped her mother and was once again abnormally interested in frozen foods. Joe Ellen took a moment to pat Tally's tee-shirted shoulder before releasing her grip. "No doubt it will be fine," she predicted, and pushed her cart around the corner.

Tally stared after her and wondered, what will be fine? Joshua and me? The kids and me? Or meeting Caroline Bangs The Drum while I'm in my grubbies? Christy, head and shoulders now buried in the frozen potato section, didn't move until Tally vanished into the next aisle.

Tally passed Mrs. Bangs The Drum and her daughters once as she dashed to get the laundry soap. She wiggled her fingers at them in what she hoped was a professional manner. It must have sufficed, for she received a nod and a smile from the great woman in return. As she checked out and wheeled her groceries to the parking lot, Tally was grateful she didn't see Jo Ellen and Christy again. I'll have to take this assimilation in small pieces, she smiled to herself. But that was love for Joshua I also saw in Jo Ellen's eyes. That was good.

She piled grocery bags on the brown velour back seat of her car, still considering her contretemps with Mrs. and Ms. Red Leggins. And Christy didn't have any homicidal weapons on her. That, too was good. But she's probably going to have a bad head cold. She guffawed aloud at the nasty thought, then quickly checked over the vinyl top of the Oldsmobile to see if anyone was observing her. Wastebasket and laser paper could wait for another day. Tally took off as fast as was legal. Already, the city girl longed for the relative security of her apartment in the heart of the reservation.

As his beloved sped toward Poplar, Joshua was poking his head into Grandfather Raymond's porch. "Shall we sweat, Grandfather?" The patriarch had a private, four-man sweat lodge in his back yard. A rustic, cold-water shower stood near it. On Saturday and Sunday mornings, and any special occasion that tickled his fancy, Raymond Wooden Headdress prayed early in the morning and started the fire that heated the rocks.

The old man was dozing in his chair and didn't awaken. Dora was probably at her own home, so Joshua slipped silently around the side of the house. The rawhide latchstring was out on the six-foot grape stake gate, which James-Dale insisted looked like the movie versions of the white man's fort. No matter, his father would tell him, it keeps us private in the sweat lodge.

Seven rocks were white hot on cottonwood embers that still flamed sporadically in a shallow earthen pit. Uniform, they were rather larger than softballs and of a pocked, volcanic roundness. Seven more sat beside a neat woodpile near the small lodge. I probably need more than a one-door sweat, Joshua thought, as he surveyed the extra rocks. He had no extra time, but he placed the second set on the fire to be ready for his grandfather. Bowing his head and extending his arms, palms up, he made formal prayer over them.

Joshua made a mental checklist. The two forked, hardwood sticks were in their proper place. He took a small bag of loose sweet grass from his shirt pocket before removing that garment and the rest of his clothes. Joshua then marched his splendid naked body to the cold-water shower, shivering as he rinsed off the top layer of the workday's grime. That done, he grabbed a denim breechcloth from one of several hooks on the side of the shower. He would cover his nudity while he carried the rocks.

Raymond's sweat lodge was small, rounded, blanket-covered. Long, bent willow poles from the banks of the Poplar were its skeleton. They formed a frame about four feet high and six feet in diameter. Hudson Bay and Pendleton wool blankets covered it, to keep the heat inside the lodge. A magnificent star quilt of crib size was a focal point on the west end of the structure, the nearest to the house.

Sweating alone, Joshua had to be his own rock-carrier. The fire-hardened sticks fit perfectly around the red-hot rocks that he knew had been blessed earlier by his grandfather. He stooped to enter the south-facing entrance, Assiniboine-traditional, according to Raymond, and was careful not to drop his burden until it was above the shallow pit in the center of the gloomy lodge. North, he prayed over the first one. Thank you, Grandfathers.

Three more trips had placed each of the four directions in the fire pit with its attendant prayer of thanks. Joshua removed the brief covering around his tan loins before he entered the sweat lodge with the seventh rock. Nude, he sprinkled sweet grass on the arrangement of rocks in the fire pit. It burst immediately into flame, filling the air with the scent of prayer. Joshua's head fell forward without volition. Thank you for my life, Grandfathers, he intoned with the fervor of gratitude, and poured the water-which-would-be-steam.

Tally was in the shower, rinsing her hair with peach essence conditioner and daydreaming of Joshua. She was through scrubbing her arms and elbows, thighs and legs with vigor and the loofah. With each stroke, she'd fantasized his hard hands on her body. She was languid from the hot water, but agitated with longing.

Three sets of clothes lay on her bed. It was three o'clock, and she still didn't know what she was going to wear to dinner at Joshua's. I can't believe I'm making such a big deal of this, she scolded herself. Wrapped in her robe, hair toweled and drying, she surveyed her final choices again.

Grandmother Headdress's brooch lay there, also. It would look well with any of the outfits, so that wasn't the problem. As she contemplated her final selections, Tally suddenly grew angry with herself. She snatched up the blue gingham blouse and matching culottes and threw them into a far corner. I wore that to the movies with Gerry Marsden, she railed at herself. I kissed him while I was wearing those clothes. Why would I even consider them? Always neat, she immediately picked up the two crumpled garments and put them carefully on a hanger. She held the offending outfit far from her body as she hung it in the rear of the closet.

A spaghetti top and matching party pajamas were spread invitingly. They were lined, apricot print on washable silk. She slipped the two pieces on her naked body and looked in the mirror behind the door. Too sexy! Too low-cut. I look like I expect to *be* the dinner, instead of coming to dinner. She removed the garments with a sigh, fondling the sensual fabric as she hung them away.

By process of elimination, Tally had arrived at her "dinner dress." It was crinkled cotton khaki pants with a soft belt of braided black and khaki cord. The matching blouse had black braiding at the collar. In a dresser drawer, she rifled through stacks of bras and panties, finally choosing a beige set. The khaki outfit went on, and the black and diamond daisy pin was magnificent at its throat. Tally wore it all as she slipped bare feet into black leather sandals and went to arrange her drying hair.

In the bathroom, she dropped minimal toiletries into her briefcase. Toothbrush, mustn't forget toothbrush! Is the underwear too sexy? What's too sexy, anyway? I don't have room for a change of clothes in here. I'll pack this T-shirt in case I spill on the blouse. What time is it? Oh, God, I have to go! She dropped her wallet in the briefcase.

Tally set her case on the kitchen floor and went back to check the patio doors. In an afterthought, she tumbled down the hallway and grabbed her new boots from the bedroom closet. Now breathless, she stood at the kitchen door again. The apartment was neat, if you disregarded the *Wolf Dancer* script lying carelessly on the corner of the kitchen cupboard

on the off chance that James-Dale might like to read it some-
day. She picked up briefcase and boots and set them outside
the door while she locked the dead bolt. Rounding the corner
below, she glanced at Gerry's apartment door and thanked
her lucky stars that he had not yet returned.

Joshua was sitting on the three-sided wooden steps at
his trailer's front door, watching for her. His upper body was
bare. Tally reveled in the dark copper of his smooth torso
and inhaled sharply at the sight of his muscular back when
he reached through the door behind him for his shirt. Rolling up the denim sleeves and tucking the tails into his jeans,
he ambled to the car to meet her. Engineer followed at his
heel.

"Have any trouble finding it by yourself?" He was handing her out of the car, looking her up and down, strangely
formal. His eyes strayed to her feet and stayed there.

"Not really. I thought I missed your private road, but then
there it was. Umm…I really didn't bring anything, Joshua…
you told me not to."

"Rattlesnake food, those pretty pink toes. No walking
beyond the clearing in those sandals, Tally Jo Carver!"

She lofted the new boots from the back seat and waved
them triumphantly, even before he was through with his ad-
monition. With her other hand, she retrieved her cowhide
briefcase. Joshua leaned over her shoulder, nuzzled her neck
in passing, and peered into the car's interior. Seeing nothing else, he looked pointedly at her briefcase and raised his
hands in mock surrender.

"Okay, but we're going to have to make a rule. No working at the dinner table, okay?" He shook his head, pretending
disbelief, and turned toward the trailer.

She moved quickly to his side. "I just didn't want to be carrying an overnight case..." She began her explanation before she saw the expression on his face. He was teasing her again! He knew what was in the briefcase. And why.

"I'll just pop the biscuits in the oven, Tally, and we can sit out here while it cools off inside." Joshua, still formal, disappeared into the interior of the trailer. As Tally lowered herself to sit on the steps, she felt the damp of the wood on the flat of her hand. Then she saw the dripping broom leaning against the aluminum exterior.

He scrubbed the steps. With a broom. Is that odd? In some manner it made her feel more at home, and she sat in peace to gaze at the little Poplar River. A bird called just as he returned to her.

"What's that bird, Joshua?"

"It's a meadowlark, dear city girl. Time was you'd hear thirty of them at a time. And we had pheasant so thick they were a nuisance. But ecological unsoundness has even caught up with us here. DDT and other pesticides. Makes the eggshells weak, I read somewhere. Fewer and fewer birds each year." He sat on a separate third of his clean front steps, the happy black and tan dog between his legs.

"Ready for some Montana cooking, honey?" He twinkled at her in that teasing manner she'd come to love.

"Ready for anything, fella. What's on the menu?"

"A little rattlesnake stir-fry. Some corn biscuits. Chokecherry jelly courtesy of Dora Moses. Rhubarb cobbler I made myself. Oh, my, I'm a fine catch. Let's eat!" He stood and extended his hand to help her rise.

She held his hand fiercely as she came to a standing position one step below him. Stepping up and into him, she asked with theatrical coyness, "Any appetizer?"

He feigned deafness as he placed both hands on her hips, backed her up, away, and through the door into the living room. "No appetizer, smart girl. But I believe I will say grace." Joshua bestowed upon her a look of purest devotion and leaned to kiss her. His mouth was at once hard and gentle, and his sweet tongue probed for answers she was all too willing to relinquish. Tally lost herself in the song of his heart as transmitted in his kiss. "Grace," he breathed hoarsely, smiled his smile and retreated into his kitchen.

Joshua tossed veggies expertly in a cast iron skillet where slivers of meat had been sautéing. He served the entrée in two portions right onto their pottery plates, poured spring water from a jug in the small refrigerator. After sitting, he jumped up and retrieved a pan of golden biscuits from the oven. "Whew!" He blew at his singed left hand and inspected the pan closely. "Nearly burned them. See what you do to me?"

Tally took her time buttering a corn biscuit, adding a thin layer of Dora's superb, tart jelly. Joshua dug into his stir-fry immediately, chewing and relishing the strips of white meat tossed with a half dozen vegetables. "Mmm. Mmm. Good." He praised his culinary skills between mouthfuls, while Tally killed time.

The stir-fry certainly smelled good, but she bought some more time by savoring her biscuit. Oh, well, she decided, if he loves it, I'll love it 'til it kills me. She gathered meat and greens on her fork and lifted it to her mouth, relished the melded flavors, then ate another forkful without comment.

"Nice dishes," she commented, when her mouth was empty. "I really like the southwestern colors." Was he disappointed as he answered?

"Rosie brought them out when I dragged the trailer from the ranch after I did the clearing. In fact, I had to stop her bringing me stuff out here. It was going to look like her parlor in a week! But I was grateful for the dishes and pots and pans and such. Another biscuit?"

They were comfortable as they ate, aware of one another, each with the same feeling. *This is so right, so just where I am supposed to be at this moment.* She ate her whole portion of the entrée without comment, and complimented him loudly and often on his cooking and his cobbler. "We had rhubarb on the Eastern Shore. My mom cooked it up in a tart sauce and made us eat it like prunes or applesauce in wintertime, for Vitamin C. I would have liked it a lot better like this!" He listened to her lilting voice without comment, loving her, overjoyed at her presence.

They took their strong, black coffee back to the steps, hoping to catch a breath of the breeze that was trying to bend the willows along the Poplar's banks. The wood slabs upon which they sat were bone dry again. "Summer solstice this coming week," Tally said aloud. "Longest day of the year."

"Always just before Red Bottom Days," he replied. "That's what it was, originally. Celebration of summer. We'll go. You'll like it."

She nodded. Of course, they'd go. Certainly, she would like it.

His voice, husky, broke the sweet silence between them again. "Pretty outfit you're wearing, Tally. Looks good with Grandma's pin. You look good in everything you wear."

She leaned back in an unconscious pose, the shirt's fabric pulling against her swollen nipples. *Oh, my God, I'm about to burst out of everything just listening to him.* Languidly, she squirmed to adjust the fit of her clothes.

"Let's take a walk," he said. "Bring Mazurka up. Settle our meal."

Grateful for the diversion, she changed into her boots. No instructions were forthcoming from his master, so Engineer gamboled excitedly around and between them on the way to Mazurka's daytime grass. A meadowlark spoke. Tally was quietly proud as she recognized the sound.

He held her hand all the way to the bend in the slow-flowing river where Mazurka had spent the day, and dropped a kiss in its palm when he left her side to unstake the filly. A rakish grin appeared at his dark mouth as he folded her hand carefully over the kiss he'd left in it. "That'll have to do you for now, honey. You okay with that?"

She rode back, holding carefully to Mazurka's mane, as Joshua's light hand on the halter guided them to the lean-to and evening treats for their four-legged family. "Whoopee!" Adrenaline pumped as she shrieked her delight at her first ride on a full-sized horse. "Oh, Joshua. Would you help me get a horse? Keep her out here? Could we go riding together? A lot? Oh, I *want* to do this!" All trace of the professional woman slipped away with the slide into his waiting arms. Immediately, she turned to stroke and utter sweet nothings to the munching filly.

"Perhaps you're only after me for my horse?" He was lighthearted again.

"Who said I was after you at all, Mr. Joshua Dale Cooks-Pretty-Good," Tally flirted. "Do you have any other qualifications?" She sat on the top of the steps again, hugging her knees, coming down from the horseback excitement.

"I make real good coffee," he bragged, "and I'm ready for another cup. You?" At her assent, he brought out two matching cups of the hot, black brew. It was six o'clock, and the cooling evening breeze began to bathe them, bringing with it the river and its willows. They leaned into it, grateful for its being, silent with their coffee and their thoughts. He spoke first, of lighter things.

"Okay, I give up. You were going to tell me. What's your first favorite thing, Tally?"

She turned her body to face him as much as possible, seated as they were on the same platform. Placing her coffee cup an arm's length from her body, she took both his hands and assumed a serious face. "I thought you could read my mind. You still don't know? It's stir-fry with pork loin strips, you terrible rattlesnake fibber!"

How she loved the brief guilty look on his face! Brief it was, for in an instant she had thrown back her head, laughed, and twisted her body around to land prone in his lap. As her round bottom rested on the top step, another look replaced the flash of guilt. Intensity, wonder, lust, amazement was in those black eyes as he lowered his mouth to hers and claimed her for all time.

Chapter Eleven

"Can I take you to my bed in the daylight?" he breathed next to her ear, his face buried in the hair at her left shoulder. "I should have a nice cross draft in there by now, and I'll be an old man by dark. Are you ready for this, Tally darlin'?"

I didn't bring any jammies. That thought tickled at the corner of her mind as she burrowed into his upper body, tasting the smooth skin of his neck. "Yes, please," she answered aloud, anxious. "Could we do that now?"

Joshua exhaled as if he'd been holding one breath for a long, long time, and his head dropped onto her shoulder for a fleet moment. Then she felt the muscles of his upper arms cord and bunch as he scooped her buttocks off the step and cradled her as if she were an infant. A wriggle achieved perfect position in his arms while he carried her across his threshold. "Guard, Engineer," shattered the silence. Tally was aroused, unable to speak.

The trip through the kitchen to his tiny bedroom was dreamlike, choreographed in slow motion by the Fates who attended them. She saw the closet and the bathroom in passing, the back of her mind registering their compactness and efficiency, her immediate attention captured by the smell of him and the iron arms that held her. A vague odor of Pinesol did sudden battle with sweet grass and was as instantly gone. Visible flush covered her body when he placed her on top of the star quilt on his bed. The sweet grass scent hung heavy there, and she was drunk with it as he released her and sat on the bed's edge.

Tally protested softly at the abandonment and reached for him. "Shh. Shh." His hoarse whisper caressed her naked ear, and he placed the slightest of tongue-kisses at the hollow of her throat. Then he pulled off her boots and turned to the task of buttons. He untied her corded belt with dexterity and slipped the tails of her shirt from the confines of its matching pants, spreading the fabric reverently about her.

Joshua buried his face in the shallow, heated depression of her upper abdomen and lay there, tasting her. She gloried in the fingertips of his left hand as they exerted upward pressure on her bottom, taking her as close to his lips as possible. Her own hands encircled his head and caressed his heavy hair, and her urgency abated as he drank of the scent of her skin.

Eyes closed and lost in the nearness of him, it didn't register for a moment that he'd ceased worshipping at her navel. He leaned over her upper body just as her eyes opened in protest, and she recoiled at the bronze face so close to her own. Soothing and smoothing the hair away from her face with one hand in that manner that melted her heart, he whispered to her. "This is close to the point of no return, dear heart. Last chance to say 'I'd rather have more rhubarb cobbler instead!'"

She managed a smile and wrapped her arms around his neck. "I've been kicking myself for two weeks that I didn't go to the buffalo wallows, whatever they are. I would never be sorry, Joshua, even if I didn't love you. And I love you so much it makes every emotion I've ever known insignificant. Now, how does this shirt come off...oh, I see, you just pull at the snaps."

With a jerk, she bared his broad, smooth chest and raised her head to kiss it and to tongue his small, square nipples. Conversation was over, if Tally Jo Carver had anything to say about it.

Joshua groaned and fell upon her as if to seal his flesh to hers. His hand beneath her back felt unsuccessfully for hooks to unfasten her brassiere. Tally insinuated her forearms beneath his chest and opened the front of her underwire bra, dropping it away from her breasts. She thought she would lose consciousness and her panties dampened instantly as she pushed the two heavy globes up against his chest. She could not stop moving against him, so desperate were her hardened nipples for the relief only he could provide. They had shared a kiss for half an eternity when he turned onto his back, reached for her hand and held it against his chest to send the message of his heartbeat.

"Would you manage the rest of your clothes, sweetheart?" Joshua was trying to speak and breathe at the same time, succeeding negligibly at both. "I'll meet you under the covers in three seconds!"

She arose reluctantly and threw her legs over the opposite side of his bed. As she pulled off one boot sock, she began to broach the subject of protection. "Er...Joshua...um, what about...you know—"

He interrupted her. "I'll take care of you, Tally. Always. I want to ride the river with you forever." He was shucking off his boots and socks as he spoke, and stood to remove his shirt and jeans. Tally had already squirmed out of her trousers and panties and now posed unconsciously, hipshot and wanton, as she turned back the quilt.

Awestruck, he was a copper statue at his first sight of her in the full-length flesh.

The wiry fluff at her mons was the color her shoulder-length hair sought to be and succeeded only in the right kind of sunlight. He thought immediately of peaches, apricots. The indentations at her waist were so endearing that his palms itched to place themselves in exactly those hollows, and her extraordinary eyes were as big and dark as an eclipse of the moon. None too soon, thought Joshua as she slipped modestly between the sheets. And even under the quilt, the lumps and bumps are all in the right places. Oh, Tally, how I love you. Please, Grandfathers, give me this.

She watched him drop his denim shirt to the floor. Late sunshine from the open skylight danced on his magnificent skin tone. His erection strained against the zipper of his Levi's and he sighed deeply as he sent the jeans after the shirt. Joshua wore no underwear, and there was something else. From his waist down, he was neither bronze nor copper-colored.

Tally sat up. She placed her hands palms outward as he came toward the bed, halting him even as her exposed round breasts begged him for succor. Her love-roughened voice was mocking, serious. "Just a minute, Joshua Dale Smith. What is this 'Indian' masquerade? That's just a deep suntan you have above your waist, from working outdoors with your shirt off. Why, your butt's as white as mine!"

Joshua backed up as far as he could in the trailer's tiny bedroom and struck a pose. Sideways he posed, chin on fist like Rodin's "Thinker," surely knowing what an awesome sight his erect manhood presented. When he was certain she had viewed his two-toned body from every angle, he extended his hands prayerfully and deadpanned to the sweet face that smiled as it demanded explanation.

"Tally, darlin', I told you I was a half-breed!" He slid into the bed and reached for her without another word.

Her body was hot to his touch, and he tossed the quilt to the foot of the bed. His left arm went under her neck as he drew her to the length of his smooth body. "Oh, oh," she moaned as she felt the firmness of his need for her. "Oh, Joshua, can we have foreplay afterwards just this once?"

He mounted her immediately. Lips covered hers with kisses that nipped and followed them with tongue that immediately healed the sting. As he slipped into the moist, slender place her desire had prepared for him, Joshua groaned his approval. Quietly, then, he stayed motionless within her, attempting to stem the urgency brought on by the feel and taste of her.

Tally's brain recorded an image of his face that she knew she would see sharply fifty years from now. The chiseled visage and eyes that had been to hell and back were a pure concentrate of his love for her, seeing everything and nothing as he absently caressed her left breast and barely moved in her. As awareness returned to his eyes, he looked into hers with such a combination of lust and devotion that sharp tears surprised her, and she let them trace down her cheeks unashamed.

When he strained to surround the erect nipple with his fierce mouth, she writhed beneath him. "Oh, oh," she moaned again, digging into his shoulders and raising her pelvis to grind against him. "Oh, Joshua, I can't wait," and she shuddered and trilled and cooed and was silent for a moment.

It was only a moment. As if he knew her from lives past, he began to move again at exactly the right time in the sweet, warm wetness. The age-old rhythm of river and prairie and sweet grass was again born anew, and the lovers went with it to the world they shared alone. At the peak of their short journey, he sobbed deep in his throat, and the muscles in his back bucked and rippled under her insensate hands. She babbled in a private language and was still as death.

There was no awkwardness as she returned to time and place. Their bodies were cooling now, still melded as one, and she scrabbled to place the sheet tenderly around his shoulders above her as protection against the evening breeze. He left tiny kisses on her eyebrows and in the hollows of her eyes, and she stretched, catlike, nearly dislodging him.

"Watch it, sweetheart," he admonished. "Things have changed rapidly up here!"

"Oh, you!" Tally grumbled and giggled and rolled his unsuspecting body off hers. She snuggled her bottom, spoon-fashion, into the warm, damp hollow with which he accommodated her. His free arm she placed across her, guiding his hand to her right breast.

"It got jealous back there," she sighed. "The other one got all the lovin'. Can you make it feel better?"

"Bathroom, honey. I'll be right back." Joshua disengaged himself from her and left the warm scent of sex and peaches reluctantly. Metal clanked and whirred, water gurgled, and then he was leaning over her. He peeled the sheet back and laved her lightly with a warm washcloth, patting her sweet, tingling regions dry with a soft hand towel.

"The hot water is tricky until you get used to it," he explained. "But don't get too fond of this kind of treatment. I'll show you how to work the water. There, isn't that better?" He dropped the pieces of terrycloth on the floor and a quick kiss on her flat belly.

"Now, where were we?" He resumed the position he had relinquished moments before. "Oh, yes, I remember." His tongue caressed her back as he urged the nipple to swell and seek his fingertips. Tally wriggled to obtain maximum friction and finally could stand it no longer. She rolled over quickly and presented the breast to his seeking mouth. He suckled to her heart's content, gently stroking the moist petals nearly hidden in that apricot haze between her thighs. When he left the breast and its rosebud nipple for a moment to investigate its twin, she protested and writhed against his hand. He barely touched her tenderest of places and found it hardened with her longing for release. He was imagining its scent and taste while he tongued a sated nipple when Tally bucked and moaned his name, drew away from him and was once again still.

Cool cotton now covered their supine bodies. She threw a leg across him and discovered his engorged condition. "Yep," he sighed. "All dressed up here and no place to go." He pantomimed clown tears and deliberately made a phallic tent of the sheet.

Propped on an elbow, she grinned mischievously. "I'll betcha I can take care of that little problem in about two minutes flat, fella. But first I want to know about all these." Tally gestured at the indented ledge that traveled three walls of the bedroom. Single condoms in several different wrappers lay in the wall nearest the bed. "Is this the 'just in case' shelf?"

"Nope." He pointed to a blue one. "That was the first one. I got it at the Texaco the night I called you. Then I got one at the Mini-Mart and one at the Exxon at Wolf Point and another at the Texaco today on the way home from work."

"But, Joshua. I've seen those dispensers. They have them in the women's room, too. They take three quarters. Don't you think all those different places knew you were buying condoms from the machine when you got quarters and went to the rest room? So, why go to all the different places?"

"Got the quarters at the change machine in the laundromat. Didn't want the moccasin telegraph to broadcast that I was buying condoms at the drugstore for the first time, the same week I took the new controller out. Didn't know how many we'd need. Doubt we have enough, though." His expression was inscrutable.

He bypassed the blue Texaco prophylactic—sentimental about the first of them, she figured—and selected the next one. "Now, there was a little matter of…" He gasped and did not finish. She had mounted him.

Impaled perfectly, it was as if she'd had years of practice in this very place. With pride in her supple body she slid up and down, round and round, back and forth on his circumcised shaft. She stretched and offered him first the left breast, then the right, elongated into heavy teardrops by her position above him. If he grew urgent beneath her, she slowed and teased, licked his nipples and kissed his mouth. When his harsh breathing quieted, she'd resume her sliding motion and give him to suck. His head rocked back and forth in agony or ecstasy, and he cupped her buttocks spasmodically with his hard hands.

Tally was again astounded. Those hands caused desire to pyramid in her every nerve ending, and soon she could not continue her rhythmic teasing. "Oh, oh," she breathed and began to tremble. Joshua groaned and rolled their joined bodies over, plunging fiercely to catch up with her, forgetting tenderness, possessing her completely. A meadowlark was delighted with the consummation and sang harmony with their contented sounds. The lovers drowsed, entwined.

She awakened quietly, luxuriantly, to a strange noise. It was wind, buffeting the side of the aluminum trailer and trying to tear into the room from the dark skylight above. Joshua was sitting up in the bed, looking down at her with the aid of two faint lights built into his bedroom wall. "Hi," she said and smiled.

"I have to stand there to shut the window above you, Tally. Scoot out for a minute, will you?"" She took that opportunity to investigate his compact bathroom.

That shower, she thought, will not accommodate two people. Too bad. "Joshua, I think I'll shower while my host makes me a sandwich or something. Do you want to show me the hot water trick?" She padded into the living room for her briefcase of toiletries, now feeling a little awkward at her nudity. When she turned to retrace her steps, he stood in the narrow hallway. His chiseled countenance was slack-jawed at the sight of her.

"By my grandfathers, Tally Jo Carver, you are purely beautiful. Are you real? I was right. There are not enough ponies on the prairie." He padded to her silently, nude and unabashed, and cupped her face as he kissed her.

"Now. I have good news and not so good news. Which first? Good? Okay. I have a Smith-built septic system to serve a six-bedroom house and last a lifetime. Thinking ahead, I was, to the time when I'd build on these forty acres."

"Well, what's the 'not so good' news, Joshua?" She stood tall and proud, her femininity reinforced by his open adoration.

"I don't have a well, honey. I haul my water in 55-gallon drums. The pump, winch, and platform are on the other side of the trailer in the generator house. Showers are, well, brief."

"Why are you going to build here if there's no water?

"No, no. Plenty of water. Not enough money. I ran out after the necessities—the septic and the road, the generator. The well was to come next spring, and I'd bring in the power the year after that. These things run into lots of dollars, Miz Accountant. But a sober man saves a lot if his woman doesn't insist on too many prawn dinners!"

She opened her mouth to ask why he said "was to come" instead of "will come," and decided against it. "Okay, show me the shower arrangement."

The turning of faucets activated the pump, and he showed her the button that warmed the water as it emerged from the showerhead. "Wet yourself down," he instructed, "and shut off the water. Soap to your heart's content, turn on the water and rinse quickly. Hair works the same way."

"Want to scrub my back?" Tally leered immodestly from the tiny, curtained cubicle as her brief allotment of warm water cascaded. She handed him her peach soap, and the new sweethearts discovered a delightful way to shower together in a one-person stall. Their yelps and happy laughter issued from the trailer and rode out on the wind to be deposited at the end of the world in lovers' nirvana.

She was clad only in the long Chincoteague tee shirt from her briefcase and brushing at her hair when he finished toweling and came to the bedroom to step into his Levi's.

"Whew! I never want to shower in there again without your help, ma'am. One sandwich, one tea, coming up."

The wind was still for a moment, and then brought rain that clattered against Joshua's cozy little home. He left her at the kitchen table and opened the living room door, which the storm immediately tried to tear from his hand. What a sight he was, barefoot and bare-chested, wrestling with the wind. "There's some small hail, Tally, in with the rain. I like the sound of the little pellets. Hope Rosie got the alfalfa all up this week. There was a lot of it cut and down when I was by there on Wednesday."

She didn't have the slightest idea what he was talking about, and didn't care. The sound of his voice fascinated Tally, as did the movement of his smooth bronze throat when he spoke. She agreed silently that the hail sound was pleasing, nodded sagely over Rosie's alfalfa, and asked small questions to keep him talking. "How big does hail get here?" "How long will a storm like this last?"

They took their cans of tea to sit on the living room couch together, christening without words each of his rooms with their combined presence. No small talk remained in them. They listened to the summer rain on the curved picture window behind them, lost in their separate thoughts. When they did speak, it was in unison.

"Will we—" she began.

"Will we—" he started. "You first, my darling." He beamed at her in the dim illumination from the walls' battery lights. "Will we what?"

"Will we have children, Joshua, is what I wanted to know?"

He enfolded her in a bear hug, his flat belly shaking with an attempt to stifle laughter. "Well, that pretty much answers my question, Tally Jo Carver. Which was 'will we be married, Tally?' Assuming you are thinking of children in conjunction with, or preferably after, marriage. To me. Yes, of course, we will be married. When?"

He had evaded her question, and she tried to keep the disheartened look from her face. As she prepared to try and put it from her mind, she remembered his lecture of just last Sunday. Those two people would have talked. Ask for an explanation before you get sad. Tally took a risk.

"Is there a reason why you didn't answer me about children, Joshua?" Her voice was soft, firm.

"Oh, honey, sorry, sorry, sorry! I got carried away with the sound of my own voice there, didn't I, planning our marriage! We will if you and the Great Spirit want us to have them, Tally. I'm prepared to build a six-bedroom house, remember?"

Tally leaned against the back of the couch and sighed, a contented smile on her face. "Okay, I won't ask you to get started on house or babies this minute. But I do get to spend the night, don't I?" She stood and yawned provocatively and dawdled her way to the bedroom. He extinguished lights as he followed her, and held her so closely in his bed that she squirmed in pain.

"Shh, there, there." She stroked his hair and whispered into his ear, as she eased his naked, iron grip. "I'm not going anywhere. I love you, Joshua." She cradled and crooned to him for long minutes.

Then she kissed him a hundred times, and he caressed her body under the tee shirt until it once again clamored for his. Joined, it was as if they had been dancing this dance for a thousand years and would perform it for a thousand more. They wrote the masterpiece slowly, perfectly, with the musical murmurs of each other's name. Joshua. Tally. The Fates smiled and blessed them each with a tear at the duet's excruciating, tender climax.

They slept like stones for hours. The pink pre-glow of sunrise had barely lightened the eastern sky when Engineer awakened them. He barked and growled incessantly, vicious outside the door.

Chapter Twelve

"Joshua! Joshua Dale! It's Christy! Aw, call your dog!"

Nude, he raced to the living room, cracked the door and spoke to the watchdog. "Down boy! Stay, good Engineer."

Tally chased him to the end of the kitchen tile, carrying his Levis. She tossed, and he pulled them on. "Christy, come in here! Christy, what's happened? The kids?"

Tally hurried back into the bedroom. The door muffled their voices, and she quickly donned her khaki pants under the tee shirt in which she'd slept. She called from the hallway. "'Scuse me. Joshua, should we make some coffee?" She was in the kitchen, barefoot and tousled, Joshua and Christy staring blank-eyed at her.

"What? What is it?" She poured spring water from the refrigerator into the coffeepot as she questioned them, unwilling to wrestle with kitchen tap water. Joshua gave Christy the floor. Her lovely almond eyes were deep and sincere as she spoke for Tally's benefit.

"I would not ever, " Christy made a gesture that took in the trailer's interior and the two of them, "deliberately embarrass or disturb you. But this was so important, I had to.

And Mom told me to get out here at first light before the cops came. I would have come sooner, but didn't think I could find it in the dark. That was in case you were here, the coming before the cops." She pointed her head toward Tally and was through with her speech.

Joshua finished making the coffee and turned on the propane burner. "James-Dale is in jail in Poplar, Tally. Someone ransacked your apartment, and a witness says he saw James-Dale coming out your kitchen door. I know old Bob Poppins, he won't move until eight o'clock. So no danger of them finding you here right now. Have some coffee and whatever before you go home. I'll go to your place when I get the boy situated.

"Situated?" Joshua paced, stormed on. "Huh! Maybe I'll kill him! Christy, any chance that he did this thing?" In the manner of all parents, Joshua was just now giving this possibility a thought.

Perking coffee and its odor seemed to lessen the tension in the trailer. Christy sat on the couch, Tally at a kitchen chair. Joshua continued to pace between them, head down. The Indian girl was quick to answer.

"I just don't think he's bent that way, Joshua Dale. He's got money. I don't think he's touched a drug of any kind since that last marijuana episode when he was thirteen. He won't even smoke cigarettes because you don't, did you know that? But maybe for spite? I don't know what goes through his head. I know he's…troubled…over you two." She sobbed now.

Christy loves him, and not just because they're family, Tally mused. Something was tugging at the corner of her mind. Something about the apartment. Christy began another heartfelt revelation, and the thought hid out in Tally's brain again, lurked there behind current events.

"But, oh, Joshua, he didn't come home until three o'clock this morning," Christy wailed. "And he won't say where he was. And…and he'd been drinking. Beer, he said. He's not booked or anything. Bob wanted to keep him at the City Building in case he decided to run away before morning. I don't think he'd do that, either." This last declaration was defiant, the she-wolf defending her pup.

"You go on home now, Christy." Joshua patted her shoulder. "I'm so grateful to you and Grandma Jo Ellen for thinking of us in the middle of James-Dale's situation." He made the same expansive gesture Christy had used, indicating himself, Tally, and the assignation in the trailer. "Tell Jo Ellen I'll be at the house five minutes after you, and we'll go to the City Building together. Okay?"

His strong hands raised Christy from the couch. "Come," he said, "I need to introduce you to Engineer, who's a pussy-cat when he knows you."

Tally heard their faint voices on the steps with the dog. She dressed quickly in the clothes she'd worn to dinner yes-terday and went to get her briefcase.

"Tally." He was in the kitchen and raised his voice to be heard through the closed bathroom door. "I'm grabbing a thermos and going to town. Take your time here, and I'll call you, or run you down if you don't stay at your apartment, when I get through with the boy."

She came into the kitchen before he was finished, for this voice was one she had not yet heard. His face was tight, angry. She advanced to hold and console him. He backed away, muttering in intense monotone. "The shoe man. Big man on the rez, you know. *He* says James-Dale did this...this vandalism. So it probably isn't going to make any difference whether he did or he didn't."

Joshua spat without moisture there in his living room, contempt so pure in the gesture that Tally shuddered. "I must go, Tally. I'll let you know when I know anything." He held her loosely for a moment, dropped the barest of kisses on her mouth, was not interested in more kissing. "I'm trying to be okay about this," he stammered, and went out the door.

Tally was stunned. She listened to the Jeep start and the crisp sound of its heavy tires on the gravel in the clearing. She heard Engineer's toenails on the wood of the steps, once again given guard duty by his departing master. Why does this make me feel like I am in the wrong, somehow?

Hot coffee remained. She poured a cup and pondered Joshua's strange actions. She stood and sipped, regarding the trailer's interior. Nothing magical here in the cold light of barely dawn, she thought, and hated herself for the negativism. I'll talk to him about it. We can talk about anything. Thus reassured, she went reluctantly through the unlocked door. "Guard, Engineer," she told the big black and tan dog, and got into her car. In fifteen minutes, if she didn't get lost, she'd know what had happened to her apartment.

Gerry Marsden's Cadillac was in its parking stall. Grateful for the early hour, Tally tiptoed up the stairs. The dead bolt was open, she knew, because it first locked, then unlocked. When the knob finally turned, Tally Jo Carver nearly fell forward into her kitchen.

Her kitchen? The little bamboo and glass table under the kitchen window was the only thing within eyeshot that looked the same as she had left it just fourteen hours ago. Two business cards lay upon it. *Robert L. Poppins, City Marshal* and *Gerald J. Marsden, General Manager.* Of course, Gerry was the representative of her landlord. She still had the spare key to give to him, new since the locks were changed. The two men had obviously been here after the reported break-in.

"Oh, no," she moaned as she surveyed the mess she could see from the doorway. All the cupboard doors were open and almost everything pulled out onto the kitchen tile. The contents of her sugar, flour and tea canisters littered the counter and spilled onto the floor. Broken dishes were going to make navigation treacherous and white footprints tracked ominously into the living room as far as she could see.

Cleaning supplies that were stored under the sink looked swept from their single file line out onto the kitchen floor. The acrid odor of ammonia came from a leaking jug of window cleaner. Aghast, Tally bent to set it upright and absently sopped at the spillage with paper towels from the floor. Thank God for plastic and paper containers, she thought. Oh, maybe I shouldn't touch anything until I talk to *Robert L. Poppins, City Marshal.*

She decided it was a very good idea, and that she'd go to the café for something to eat. Treading carefully, she charted her course carefully through the living room to check the lock situation on the French doors. Two strange, wood folding chairs were jammed under the knobs. The vandals must have gotten in through here. If the chair-locks were good enough for the marshal, they were good enough for her. Tally went to breakfast.

The Poplar Café was open from six to eight, seven days a week, the sign said. It was 6:10, and a woman in street clothes came to open the door just as Tally tried and found it locked. "Running late today," she said. "Usually nothing happens 'til eight or so on Sunday. Counter?"

"I'd really like to sit in a booth, since you won't be busy. Is that okay?" The waitress was tying a big, white, triangular apron around her ample waist. She gestured to the row of early morning clean booths at right angles to the door.

"Help yourself, ma'am," she answered. "I'll bring a breakfast menu, and the first coffee is just coming down." Clangs and clatters came from the bowels of the kitchen. A cook presumably waited for Tally's order.

"Oh, thanks. Coffee as soon as possible, okay?" Tally slumped in the booth, head in both hands, envisioning the mess she had just left and dreading the vandalism she had not yet seen. She decided she would not think about Joshua and his changed attitude just now.

Tally killed an hour with bacon and eggs and the Sunday paper, which came to Poplar on Saturday night. I'll go on home and check my jewelry, she decided, because when I call the marshal at eight, he'll probably want to know what's missing. Why would James-Dale trash my house? Say, where's the *Wolf Dancer* script?

Tally visualized the wreckage in the apartment. No, it wasn't on the counter with the spilled foodstuffs. She decided to look for the script the minute she got back to the apartment. With a purpose now, she quit dawdling, paid her check and started home, a large coffee-to-go in a bag. The café was empty all the while she ate, but as she backed out of her parking space a big car pulled in beside her. It was Gerry, and she couldn't avoid him.

The tall man got out and scurried to her window, which she opened reluctantly. "Come and have breakfast with me,

Tally, so you don't have to face your apartment alone. You do know about it, don't you? I am just sick for you. Where have you been?"

"I've been home already, Gerry. I'm fine with it alone, and I just had breakfast. I thought I shouldn't clean up anything until I talk to the marshal. About eight o'clock, I figure? Yes. Well, then, I'm just going to go home and tiptoe through the rooms, trying to figure out what's missing."

"It was the lawn-mowing kid, Tally. That Smith's son. I got a good look at them when they left your place. It was about ten o'clock last night, just as I got home. I stayed in Billings for some dinner." Gerry was self-involved this morning, but not enough to repeat his question about where she had been.

Tally escaped him and hurried to the apartment, knowing he would be underfoot as soon as his breakfast was over. She would have to cooperate with him as the landlord's representative. *What did he said about James-Dale? Damn! I wasn't listening to him, just trying too hard to get away. Something...*

If anything, it was worse than she'd thought during her first observation. Tampons and the contents of her sewing box littered the hallway. Under-the-sink supplies nearly obscured the bathroom floor, and the shower curtain dangled, half its hooks forlorn on the steel rod. There was no lid on the toilet tank. By the time she reached her bedroom, Tally was numb to the chaos.

She wanted to sink, to sit and cry forever. Instead, she called on her indomitable spirit and crept into the carnage. Everything in the closet seemed to be on the carpet or hanging on the mattress that stood, cockeyed, beside the bed. The tall, maple jewel chest was noticeably absent from the dresser and her hand jerked to her throat. Grandma Wooden Head-dress's pin was there, at her throat. "Whoosh!" Accumulated breath in her lungs released itself in relief. One way to get rid of Dougie's wedding set. Giggles were uncontrollable at the incongruous thought, and Tally spoke to herself sharply.

"Do not get hysterical, Thalia Josephine Carver! Nobody's dead. A mess is just…a mess, and can be cleaned. Insurance replaces theft. And if James-Dale did this, well, we'll work it out. Now, what time is it?" It was quarter 'til eight, and she was done with sightseeing. Back at her uncluttered kitchen table, Tally Jo Carver drank cooling Poplar Café coffee, looked out at Montana and waited for eight o'clock.

She was on the phone with the marshal's office when Gerry Marsden and eight o'clock arrived together. The deputy said Bob was waiting for her call, and he'd have Bob get right up there, probably after breakfast. He also asked where she had been when the break-in occurred. Tally said thanks, she would wait for the marshal, and ignored his question as she hung up the phone and greeted her landlord at the screen door.

"Oh, Gerry. Here, let's talk outside." She went onto the outside walkway with her paper cup of coffee. "It's so depressing in there. You don't really have to be here, of course. Your people have no liability, and I have renter's insurance."

"Well, I can smooth the path for you, Tally. I know Bob Poppins well. He does a good job keeping this town in line."

Gerry droned away as Tally had an instant thought at the tone of his voice. I'll bet next week's paycheck that Bob Poppins is not an Indian marshal.

"…and you can be comfortable while you wait," he was saying, looking at her expectantly. She rolled back the tape in her subconscious and heard him asking her to his apartment. She could hardly refuse the neighborly gesture.

"I don't want to miss the marshal," she answered hesitantly.

"I'm sure he'll check in with me first," Gerry replied. "C'mon, I put in French Roast coffee beans last time I shopped, just for you!"

Tally looked at her watch. When will Joshua come? Well, I need to tell Gerry about Joshua, anyway, so guess I'll get some decent coffee. "Okay, Gerry. Let's go."

He opened his door and stepped in to a twin of Tally's kitchen. He held the door for her, his tall body stretching to steady the screen. She stooped to enter.

Joshua saw her khaki pants ducking under Marsden's arm just as he pulled the Jeep to the curb. His face tightened as the shoe man's door closed. He sat for two minutes and pulled away slowly when she did not reappear. It was now after eight, and Jo Ellen wanted to go to the City Building.

Bob Poppins' official car pulled to the same spot at the curb just as the Jeep went out of sight around the southwest corner. He opened and closed the chain link gate and walked straight to Apartment 1-A. Gerry Marsden answered as soon as the marshal rapped. "We're waiting for you, Bob. Come on in."

"Pleased to meet you, Miz Carver," the marshal said officially. "Where were you when the break-in occurred?"

"I was with friends." Tally made it an offhand comment, and went on immediately. "My jewel box is missing. Nothing valuable, except a third-carat diamond ring, some gold earrings and a gold bracelet. Could we do whatever you have to do in the apartment, so I can start cleaning up the mess?"

Is the marshal actually looking at Gerry for guidance, to know whether he should pressure me to learn exactly what "friends"? Gerry must have a little class, anyway, since no one is asking further. "And do I have to sign a complaint or anything?" Tally was on her feet and ready to go upstairs.

"What can I do to help you, Tally?" Gerry was the epitome of good neighbor and concerned landlord.

"A couple of trash cans right outside my door, I think, Gerry," she answered immediately, for Tally's brain had been making a plan to put her apartment back in shape all the while she was drinking coffee. "And keep that wonderful coffee hot, I guess. Thanks, Gerry. You're a good friend." She opened the door, the marshal right behind her. Gerry stood, realized he had no invitation, and sank back into his easy chair.

"Let's start with the jewel box, Miz Carver." Bob Poppins was professional, surprising her. "Where did you keep it?" They were moving gingerly through the debris, and Tally led him down the hall and into her bedroom.

"On the short dresser there," she pointed to a corner obscured by the bed's placement. The marshal donned surgical gloves as he stepped carefully through the clothing on the floor.

"Probably won't need to take fingerprints, since we've got the kid," Poppins said. "But I should practice good work at all times, just in case." His smile was not quite sheepish as he explained.

Oh, my God. James-Dale! How could I have forgotten? Oh, Joshua. Tally's heart groaned, and she opened her mouth to speak of it to the marshal just as that thorough man raised the tall, slender jewel box from the floor.

"This it, ma'am?" The box he held was virtually empty. A couple of mismatched earrings were stuck to the velvet in the rear of the bottom shelf. One of its doors dangled on a single hinge.

"Oh, I didn't look behind the bed. Yes," she peered around the end of the four-poster at the space where the marshal was carefully standing. "And there doesn't seem to be any jewelry on the floor there, does there? So, that's what they took."

"Well, ma'am, Mr. Marsden has identified the boy, the Smith kid who mows the lawn here. He saw him leaving the apartment." Poppins was stepping gingerly past her out of the bedroom now, peeling off one latex glove. "Anything else missing, do you think?"

Tally looked around the bedroom. "I had a brand new star quilt folded on the end of the bed here. I don't see it on the floor. Could we move this mattress here? Why do you think James-Dale Smith, a boy whom I know—as well as his father and his sister—would trash my house and stand this mattress on end? It doesn't sound logical to me." Tally was adamant.

"Has he been here, Miz Carver? In your apartment?"

"Well, yes. We all looked at a movie one night."

"Gosh, ma'am. Who can figure kids these days? We've never had a speck of trouble with this one. Hard-working like his dad, I always figured. Like I said, who knows, these days? But Mr. Marsden saw him, so that's pretty much that." The marshal was ready to leave, hand on the kitchen door.

"What does James-Dale say, Marshal Poppins?" Tally needed to know. *I am deeply in love with his father,* she wanted to say. *I don't want to believe James-Dale would do this to me.*

"My weekend deputy picked him up, ma'am. Late—late last night. I haven't seen him yet. I'll try to get your property back, and will let you know." The marshal was gone. Tally listened at the door, and heard him stop at apartment 1-A.

She found sweat pants and a tee shirt on the bedroom floor. She wrapped the brooch in tissue and placed it lovingly on the bottom of her briefcase, and tears started again. "Stop it, Tally! Get to work!" she chastised herself aloud. What would be was going to be, and it was just not possible that Joshua would let this come between them. Not now.

She started with the smallest room. The top of the toilet tank was in the tub in two jagged pieces. It had made an ugly gash in the enamel. The pieces were heavier than they looked, and she carried them carefully through the kitchen to sit outside the kitchen door. For the trash, she thought, and Gerry will need to know that I need a new one.

In the kitchen she had to give up on the idea of making her own coffee; the grounds were strewn from the vacuum jar all over the flour and sugar, tea bags, crackers, and oatmeal packets that littered the floor. She considered going down and getting a tall cup of Gerry's French Roast, and decided she didn't want coffee that badly. Instead, Tally popped the top on a can of tea and went back to the bathroom, methodically salvaging what she could. Two hours passed quickly, and she had worked her way out to picking up tampons in the hallway when there was a knock on the door.

Oh, please. Please be Joshua, Tally said to herself. Her disappointment was probably obvious to Gerry Marsden, who stood at her screen door with a tall thermos cup of coffee. His own cup was in his other hand.

"Bet you can use this by now, Tally." He smiled and came in without invitation, extending his welcome gift. "I thought

I saw your coffee spilled all over the kitchen floor yesterday. Want to take a break?"

She thanked him profusely and crossed past him to go out into the air, away from the wreckage of her apartment. She sat on the top step and drank the good coffee, listening to his platitudes, waiting to tell him of Joshua and ask about James-Dale. "What I really need, Gerry," she began, and didn't get a chance to finish. The Jeep screeched to the curb and an angry Joshua stalked through the gate.

"Up here, Joshua!" She called to him with familiarity, anxious for the other man to know the extent of the relationship.

"I'm looking for Marsden—oh, there he is!" Joshua took the steps two at a time, his booted feet echoing on the covered, wooden stairway. "Marsden, what the hell is going on?"

Gerry was smooth, secure, but not anxious for trouble with the angry Indian father. "About the boy, do you mean, Smith?"

"What else would I mean?" Joshua shot a glance at Tally as he said this. He stood at the top of the stairway, fists clenching and unclenching at his sides. His eyes met Tally's, and his face softened a little. The voice that made her tremble was calmer when he spoke again.

"Mr. Marsden, James-Dale is home with his grandmother on my word as bond. He swears he's only been in Tally's apartment the once, and did not break in or vandalize it last night. I believe him, but what's more important, his grandmother believes him. You are going to have to re-think your identification of him."

"I'm sorry, Smith. I have teenagers, too, so I know how you must feel. But I saw them quite clearly, the boy in particular. He had a bundle in his arms and was coming out of Tally's door. It was your boy, all right. Skinny, black hair, beaded headband, jeans. The outside lights were already on."

"What do you mean—*them*? Who was he with? Did you identify the other kid?" This was the first Joshua had heard of another vandal. Tally's head was working overtime, for she had heard Gerry say 'them' once before, and let it go right past her.

"Looked like a girl," Gerry said, anxious to keep Joshua calm. "Remember, it was dusk, but I had the distinct impression it was a blonde girl. Not…not Indian," he stammered.

Joshua shook his head in disbelief. "There's no white girl James-Dale would be out running around with on a Saturday night. Now I know for sure he didn't do it. Not that I didn't believe him!"

Tally interrupted them. It was a good time to intercede, while both were conversing in a normal tone of voice. Her choice of words was unfortunate. "I'm sure Gerry thinks he saw James-Dale—" she began.

"And I'm not so sure, Tally! I think all Indian kids with beaded headbands look alike to Mr. Marsden, and this is not going to get pinned on my son!" His gesture was age-old. *I have spoken. So be it.*

"I need to talk to Joshua alone, Gerry. Thanks for the coffee. I hope you'll think it over, now that it's pretty sure that James-Dale didn't—" Her words chased him as he hurried down the stairway. Gerry Marsden was glad to be dismissed from the confrontation.

"Come on in, Joshua, I think I might have an idea," Tally said, and led the way into the kitchen. She reached for his hand, but Joshua sidestepped her, even as he gasped at the carnage visible from the door.

"I don't want to take this out on you, Tally. But that smug bastard isn't fit to touch your hand, and you cozy up to him every chance you get, even when his bigoted mouth is harming my family." His face was a storm cloud as he stopped in the open screen door and went on. "What am I supposed to think? It's the same old thing. Red and white just do not mix on the reservation, Tally. There's always trouble!"

"Oh, no, Joshua. You're just angry with Gerry. He's a fool. But he's my landlord. And neighbor. But you and I—we mix, Joshua. We're going to ride the river forever, remember?"

His face held two hundred years' sorrow. "I'm afraid I led you on, Tally. I am sorry for that. I apologize for letting my passions get in the way of my better judgment. I prayed, and I thought I had an answer. But this—this kind of thing will always happen. And I had my family—my children—first. I am afraid nothing can come of us. Forget it!" He whirled and was gone.

Too wounded to weep immediately, her first inane words were, "I'll just pick up the big chunks here in the kitchen…" The dishwasher pellets, Ivory Liquid, and Windex were intact, and she put them back on the shelf under the sink, while silent tears flowed. Room deodorant and duster spray cans were scattered a little farther along, and she sobbed as she stepped carefully to retrieve them. Familiar, bold, black writing caught her eye, nearly covered with flour and sugar.

She picked up the stained cover and first six pages of *Wolf Dancer*, ripped from its brads and tossed away as if worthless. She knuckled her eyes, too intent on her discovery to cry any longer. Yes, that was another section there near the living room. Her mind's eye replayed the scene where James-Dale Smith held the script in his hands. Reverently, he had held it.

Joshua's *chos-kay* did not do this, she thought, and went to the phone. It rang as she placed her hand on it.

Chapter Thirteen

"Tally? That you, Tally?" Doug Holcomb's voice came across the phone wire. She could see his sheepish face and the brown hair spilling onto his forehead, recognized his apologetic tone.

He's having second thoughts about Montana, she chortled to herself. "Oh, Doug. Are you okay? Where are you?"

"Cincinnati, Tally. Came to my senses here, I think. It isn't going to do me any good to go out to Montana, is it?"

"Oh, Doug, no. I was so sure I made that clear to you when I was getting ready to leave."

"Oh, honey, I know. I just have been so used to having you here when I needed to bounce my stuff off you. I guess I have to grow up some, huh?"

Tally was overjoyed to hear his acceptance and ventured some levity. "Yeah, and if you'd get a bimbo with brains, Doug, then you'd have a bouncer-offer, too!"

He roared into the Cincinnati phone receiver as she continued. "But you must have got your messages to have my phone number. Here's the help I need. Ready to write? Okay, now, you roomed with Carroll Larksmond III at school. He's on the General Counsel's staff of the Valu-Wear Shoe

Company up in Connecticut. I saw his name on a picture. Well, here's what I want you to do…" Tally went on, ending with, "This is real important to a lot of people, Doug. Thanks for your help."

Her ex-husband seemed to have matured considerably during his short trip. "Glad to help you, Tally. Sometime, I'll visit Montana. You be happy there, okay? I'll call you Monday as soon as I know anything. Right now, I have to turn around and drive back to D.C.!"

Her next call was to the marshal's office. The deputy asked if she couldn't call Bob tomorrow, Monday. "No, deputy, it's too important. You get hold of him and tell him I want fingerprints from this jewel box. I want to talk to him now."

Tally peeked into the bathroom once again, rejoiced in one tidy space, and set about finishing the hallway. She was in the spare room closet, wrestling with the vacuum cleaner, when someone beat on the kitchen door. She figured it was Gerry again and went grudgingly to answer it.

Blue Cloud Ransome stood there, two huge grocery boxes at her side and a pair of pink rubber gloves in one hand. She was clad in her gardening overalls. "Bet you could use a little help here, Miz Carver?" Looking beyond Tally at the kitchen, she squealed with something that sounded like joy. "Oh, my, I guess you can!"

They put one box in the kitchen, one in the living room, and bent to the task. Blue Cloud was a prodigious worker. She didn't talk. Occasionally, she raised something that she might salvage into the air. Tally pointed to garbage box or sink, and the happy waitress would either toss it to hear it smash, or place it gently in the kitchen sink for cleaning and replacement on a shelf.

The two women made an amazing dent in the kitchen-living room area in an hour and a half, and Tally was pleased. "Whew! Look at what we've accomplished! My mom used to say, 'many hands make the work lighter.' Isn't it a gift that they didn't break my little glass-front curio case there? Shall we go down to the café for some lunch? And, Blue Cloud, please—always call me Tally. Okay?"

"Tally, I can't stop for lunch. Got a cold drink? I have to get home and get stuff ready for the kids for Vacation Bible School tomorrow, and iron a couple things for my husband. I'll take this kitchen box down to empty in the dumpster right now, before it gets any heavier, then I'll take a bottle of pop. If the back of the house isn't any worse than this was, we can be done in another two hours, I betcha!"

"Actually, I've got the bathroom and—" Her take-charge visitor was out the door before Tally had finished, dragging the box of broken dishes and mistreated foodstuffs with her. Tally was staring after her in wonderment when the phone rang. This time it was Marsden.

"Anything I can do for you, Tally? I see you've got some help up there now. That's good."

He's just too pompous to live! She found herself angry with him and was amused that she wasted the energy.

"No, nothing, Gerry." Disgust was undisguised in her tone as she went on. "And you can forget about the garbage cans, because Blue Cloud brought me some big boxes, and I'm sure Joshua will haul the trash away for me. I have to get off the phone, because I'm waiting for the marshal to call. 'Bye."

He was still sputtering his sorries about the trash cans when she set the receiver gently in its receptacle and went to get Blue Cloud a Pepsi. Not at all sure that Joshua will be hauling my trash or anything else, she thought, but that should let Gerry Marsden know where I stand. Where he stands.

She wanted to know so many things, but was determined not to grill the splendid, round woman across the table from her. Blue Cloud was in a hurry to return to the cleanup and drank noisily from her can of Pepsi. Even then, she was a vision of serenity to her companion. Tally ventured a question. "I guess the moccasin telegraph is why you came?"

Blue Cloud's laughter pealed as she stood and began to take the broom to the kitchen floor. "You catch on to the reservation fast, Miz—er, Tally! That's what it was, all right!"

"Well, does the moccasin telegraph know who did this?" Tally stood and prepared to go to her bedroom.

The Indian woman went still in mid-stroke, broom outstretched, and looked directly into Tally's eyes across the room. "No. And they know who didn't do it, too, Tally."

Chills ran from Tally's scalp to both elbows at the fervor in Blue Cloud's voice. Silenced, she went to tackle her bedroom.

Blue Cloud followed, peering into the white-walled room, knee-deep in littered clothing. "How about if I hang up these clothes and such, Tally, and you take the other room? The papers and so on. None of the computer glass is broken, so I guess that's lucky."

Before she exchanged rooms, Tally threw a tea towel over the jewel chest. "I want Marshal Poppins to take fingerprints from it," Tally explained. "Let's not put any more prints on it while we're cleaning."

Blue Cloud had the mattress in place and was vacuuming its cover when Tally finished with the minor damage in her home office. Some separate stacks of underwear and tee shirts lay folded on the low chest, ready to place in ravaged dresser drawers, and all the clothes that littered the floor were now on hangers in the double closet.

"Hey!" Tally shouted over the vacuum, waving a hand. Blue Cloud shut it off immediately. "Hey! We've got all the hard work done. I can't tell you, Blue Cloud, what it means to me to have you come help me. I'd have cried and waded through it forever." This was probably not true, but she wanted the woman to know how much she appreciated the demonstration of friendship. "You go on home now. I can do the vacuuming and straightening after I rest a while."

Blue Cloud left the bedroom unceremoniously, stripping her rubber gloves as she went. Tally followed the Indian woman, who stood and surveyed the neat kitchen with its swept floor, a contrast to the white smears that still marred the living room carpet. "Yeah, there's not much left. I'll go ahead and go." She lingered yet a moment. Finally, she blurted it out. "My husband is white, Tally. It's hard, and you have to make a hundred per cent commitment. A hundred per cent on each side. It averages out to fifty-fifty that way. In the beginning, nothing else can matter. We have been married seventeen years now, and it is more than fine. We're just… married people."

She was not going to speak of Joshua and Tally, or any current happening. Blue Cloud was through with her speech and turned to leave. Tally ran quickly to the curio cabinet and selected a six-inch cut glass vase. She took Blue Cloud's two hands and placed the antique treasure carefully in their center. "Thank you for honoring my home," she said formally. "This was my great-grandmother's."

Understanding and appreciation showed in Blue Cloud's eyes as she thanked Tally in the same, formal manner. "The honor is mine, Tally. We will all be family, I think." Her smile was brilliant as she hurried away to her children and her ironing.

Gerry Marsden, on the verge of exiting his apartment, closed the door quickly and remained inside until Blue Cloud was gone from the stairs.

Tally sat down to a quick snack. Head in her hands, she relived his arms, his mouth, the strength and smell of him as he moved above her. Just last night? Surely, it can't be over? Her thighs clenched as the memory of Joshua took over, and she cursed the telephone when it interrupted her fantasy.

"Bob Poppins here, Miz Carver. I was out fishing. Got a couple nice walleye. You want fingerprints?"

"I'm certain James-Dale Smith didn't do this, Marshal. How it appears, remember? Like they were looking for something? Joshua Smith told me that some 'unsavory people' lived here before me. Could they have been drug dealers?" When the marshal opined they might have been just that, she went on.

"Well, my apartment looks like the vandals were looking for dope. A skinny Indian youth with a beaded headband and a white girl in tow was here Saturday morning. His name was something like Come Along. Xavier, for sure."

"Goes Along, probably. I think they have a kid named Xavier, been gone a while, just got back to the rez a couple of months ago. How did you happen to get his name?"

"He told me, Marshal Poppins." Here, she stretched the truth. "But he looked like a strung-out doper to me, and I've seen a lot of them in the city where I come from. I want you to find him and see if he has my things. And if you won't do that, I want fingerprints off this chest, because I'm sure you won't find James-Dale's on it." Tally was firm and would not be denied when she was in her controller mode.

"We do have the eyewitness, ma'am," Marshal Poppins began.

Tally went ballistic on the phone over his bureaucratic nonsense. "Marshal, are you elected or appointed?"

"Er, appointed, Miz Carver. Why would you ask?"

"Because if you don't give me some immediate satisfaction—either by picking up the Goes Along boy with some of my property, or getting his fingerprints off my jewel chest—I'm going to call my boss. Ezra Bangs The Drum. The Chairman, the Chief of the Tribes. You've heard of him?"

"I will do good police work, Miz Carver. And, since you think there's a chance it could be the other youth, well… of course, I'll look into it." He was anxious to get back to a working relationship with no more references to the tribal chairman. "I'd better get right on it. My son can clean the fish."

Tally took a deep breath. "I'll apologize in person for the threat, Marshal Poppins. But it's too important to James-Dale and his family not to get on it immediately, before any evidence gets lost. Now, one last thing. Can you send someone to fix the locks on my patio doors? Under the circumstances, I don't want to ask Joshua Smith."

Tally went to bed before midnight Sunday, with a tidy apartment and an aching heart. She felt safe enough. There were new sliding bolts drilled into the floor in front of the French doors, sturdy enough to withstand a battering ram. The workman who came late that Sunday to do the job made an astute observation. "Those finials, ma'am. On the corner posts of the railing? Not a good idea. Somebody threw a loop on one, no doubt, and skinnied his way up to your deck, then pushed through these candy-ass doors. 'Scuse my French, ma'am."

Tally didn't know what a "finial" was—the decorative tip on just about anything that stretched upward, she learned later from the dictionary—but agreed to their removal. He volunteered to come back Monday evening and do the work. "Get an okay from Mr. Marsden in 1-A, will you?" Talley said. "Value-Wear is my landlord." He promised it would be done.

She retreated to her bed after a long, soaking bath. The sweet grass from her car now graced her bed's headboard. Its scent comforted her, though she shed a few more tears before falling asleep. *Joshua will call me tomorrow,* she hoped. *It will be all right.*

The moccasin telegraph had been busy. Her staff gathered round her on Monday morning, commiserating and asking if there was anything any one of them could do. Bob Wilson heard of her robbery when he got to work and was so solicitous she had to reassure him often that she was fine, just fine. Joshua did not call.

Nor had he called at home or at the office by Tuesday, when Tally got a call from her ex-husband just as she was getting ready to leave the office. He had the information she'd asked him to get, and she jotted a few notes. "Thank you, oh so much, Doug. This is a good thing you've done." She went to stand over the noisy fax machine to insure privacy for the pages he was transmitting to her as soon as the conversation was finished. She looked those pages over, made a couple of notes, and locked them in her briefcase.

Bob Poppins called soon after she walked into her apartment Tuesday after work. "His girl hitched out of Poplar Monday morning, Miz Carver, and I picked up Xavier Goes Along at his mother's house. He denies being in your apartment and gave me his prints voluntarily. So the eyewitness report will stand for now, ma'am."

"Until you fingerprint the box, Marshal, right?"

"Oh, right. Of course, Miz Carver. I'll come over right now, if that's all right, and send a car to Billings with the prints in the morning."

It was, of course, all right with Tally. She would have a visit with Mr. Gerald Marsden as soon as she cleared it with Ezra. She was certain Gerry would not be so quick to identify James-Dale as the burglar when she was through talking to him.

She patted the briefcase on the floor beside her. She had a surprise for Mr. Marsden.

Chapter Fourteen

The buzz in the office on Wednesday was all about Red Bottom Days. The dance prizes were monsters, they chattered. $1000, $500. There were more vendors setting up than they'd ever had before. Dancers were expected from Michigan and Minnesota as well as Canada, North and South Dakota, Wyoming, and Nebraska. Most of the accounting staff were single women, and they giggled about their new outfits and the boyfriends they had or wanted to attract. Marian Moses continued to remind them that it was a workday.

"We get a little heady every year at this time, Tally," she explained to her boss at midmorning. "It's a really big deal, Red Bottom Days. Are you going?"

"Yes, I want to go, Marian. I saw the area where they hold it. It's outside, so it won't be too crowded, will it?" Tally hid her few weaknesses carefully. She didn't want to miss the festival, but crowds were her least favorite thing.

"Well, the parking gets pretty hairy, Tally. Other than that, there seems to be room for everyone. It crowds up around the dancers during the contests. People bring stools and chairs." Marian waited at the side of Tally's desk, for response or dismissal.

"I think I'll go Friday after work." Tally forced gaiety. "I'm going to eat one of everything at the food stands and watch some of the dancing. What's more, anyone who wants to take the afternoon off Friday can owe me two hours in January." She heard the yelp of pleasure from her staff as Marian relayed the news.

Tally maintained an attitude of lightheartedness she did not feel. I still have a date, she hoped. Joshua said we'd go. He said, of course, we'd go. So, of course, we will. She looked at the phone on her desk for the umpteenth time that morning. The Billings lab would process the fingerprints today, and she'd hear from the marshal. Would she hear from Joshua?

At home that evening, she sat out on her tiny deck in the molten sun, trying to warm bones grown cold with fear in the days since Sunday. Have I thrown my heart into the ring with a capricious fool? Again, she had a long talk with herself, scolding her faint heart for its lack of faith in the monumental thing that had happened with Joshua Smith. Yet, when the phone rang at seven, she knew it was only the marshal.

"That whacked-out kid's fingerprints are all over your jewel box, Miz Carver. My deputy picked him up about an hour ago, just lying around his mother's house. He says he used the diamond and the star quilt to get crack cocaine from the local dealer. He still hasn't told us who the dealer is, and I doubt he will. The girl has hitched out of town with the rest of your jewelry, ma'am. We put her on the wire, but I wouldn't be hopeful. He didn't even know her name. 'Woman,' he said. 'Woman is her name.'"

"Good work, Marshal Poppins. I appreciate you clearing James-Dale Smith's name. You'll call his grandmother right away, I hope?" Tally was polite, and hopeful that this turn of events would help smooth the way for Joshua to get back to her.

"No offense, Miz Carver, but I called old Jo Ellen War-bonnet first. She's been burning up the telephone wires, you know. I would sure want her on my side if I was ever in any trouble! And that goes for you, too, ma'am. Again, no offense meant, but I sure would want you on my side." He chuckled and said goodnight just as the sound of the big Cadillac pull-ing into its parking space filtered through the open French doors.

Tally was in a robe, changed from her office outfit. Now she slipped into jeans, a tucked-in tee shirt, and the light-weight blazer she had worn on the plane to Montana less than three weeks ago. She glanced into the bathroom mir-ror. Satisfied that her professional air was about her, she gave him time enough to get into his apartment. Then she took her briefcase and went below to finish with Mr. Marsden.

"I'm on business, Gerry." Tally brushed off his insinceri-ties about her ordeal, how she was holding up, and how nice it was to see her smile again. The façade of his handsome face melted away, and he was uncomfortable. It was obvious that control was his only position of choice. Well, she had no time to feel sorry for him right now.

"Gerry," she began, as she opened her briefcase slowly, "did I tell you I'm acquainted with Carroll Larksmond III? On your general counsel's staff? 'Junior, Junior,' we call him. I have Valu-Wear's last profit and loss statement here. Branches, and in toto."

He slumped at the kitchen table. "Aw, Tally. Isn't that some kind of a breach of something? Why would you do that?"

"Well, first I wanted to see if you were bleeding the Tribe for nothing—a nice cushion, $24,000 a year. You get a 1099, so I expect you have paid the taxes on it? Then, when I *knew* you were—extorting, I mean—I was going to induce you to take another look at your identification of James-Dale Smith. Because I was pretty sure it was a doper kid and his girl who broke in."

Gerry scraped his chair away from the white Formica-topped butcher's table and began to pace the kitchen floor.

"I guess I don't have to show you these financial reports, do I, Gerry? You know what I'm talking about. The home office is very, very happy with the profits from the Ft. Peck factory. And with your management of it, I might add. They would never think of closing it."

He stopped in the center of the kitchen floor, his face grown old in these few minutes. "Tally, believe me. The first year and a half, I had to beg to keep it here. They quit expanding westward and thought we should just fold up here, too. That's when the inner council gave me the monthly money for all the extra work I did to keep the factory here. I just got used to the money, Tally. Child support and alimony and all three kids to put through college—"

She waved a hand at him, brushing away the sound of his whine. "And Cadillacs, and eating out every meal, and only you know how much you've salted away, Gerry. Well, let us agree right now that it's over. That if Valu-Wear should move without a real valid reason anytime in the next few years, its management will know of your extortion at Fort Peck." She was coldly professional, getting the job done, leaving out no detail. Her stone gray eyes reduced him to a whimper in neatly pressed Dockers.

"Okay, Tally. Sure. It was time, anyway. I just kept putting it off. Sure. No more money from the Tribes."

"That's it, then, Gerry. We won't speak of it again." Tally rose to go and told the end of the break-in story almost as an afterthought. "The fingerprints of a boy named Xavier Goes Along are all over my jewel box, and the marshal has him in custody. He's a skinny addict with a beaded headband, two or three years older than James-Dale. And doesn't resemble him in the least, either. I've only seen each of them once, and I know that much. If I were you, Gerry, I'd take a hard look, deep down where your identification of the burglar came from."

She left him there, penitent and defeated. Upstairs on her diminutive deck, she sipped at a can of tea and looked at the empty patio chair in the opposite corner. What fun she'd had picking out the two from the limited supply at the trading post, and Joshua had never sat in his. Yet. Tally took the three small steps to the other chair and sat sideways in it, face against the bright canvas. She could not smell sweet grass any longer, and her shoulders soon heaved with silent sobs. She hurried inside to run water at the bathroom sink to ensure that no one heard.

Tally dressed carefully on Thursday in a lightweight power suit, worn to important meetings in her Washington, D.C. days. A matching teal band pulled her hair from her face and turned her uncommon eyes ice green. She took Grandmother Headdress's daisy pin from the bottom of her briefcase, thought better of it, wrapped and replaced it. No jewelry suited the aura she was trying to exude. A professional woman, first and foremost, was Tally Carver today.

Thursday was Camping Day at the Red Bottom Festival. She learned about it from the mature clerk, painfully shy

Tammy Runsbelow. "I didn't think to ask you yesterday, Miz Carver? It's Camping Day? The youth? They do the feast at five and the whole powwow, starting at seven. I've got two boys and a girl in it, two of 'em dancing. I'd like to take my half day today instead of tomorrow?" Tammy delivered all this information while staring at a yellow pad on the desk.

Tally wanted to chuck Tammy's chin until the woman looked up at her, but she just agreed to the change in days, with thanks for the information. As she turned away, Tammy murmured restrained thank-yous.

Sarah Grey Wolf, a vocal and talented woman of twenty-three years, spoke loudly at Tally's retreating back. "Great outfit, Ms. Carver. Really wham-mo!"

Not feeling very 'wham-mo,' she said to herself, as she leaned on the inside of her closed office door. I have a lot of work to do, preparing for the end of the 2nd quarter, and Joshua will either come or call today, or he will not. But I can handle either one. She called on her work ethic to sustain her and waded into her tasks with the same spirit she'd begun the Herculean job in her trashed apartment.

Tally ended the day with a stack of quality output, grateful again that she loved her work. The offices were empty except for Bob Wilson, who stuck his head in at 5:30. "Racing off, boss lady. Want me for anything?"

A shake of her head and a fluttered, small wave dismissed him. Now she was, indeed, alone. She had not heard from Joshua and must sit quietly and make a decision.

She did, and found herself driving to the other end of Poplar. She parked in front of the oddly placed arbors that created Grandfather Raymond's atrium entrance. Honeysuckle was blooming on several, its scent so fragrant in the warm afternoon air that it warned how cloying it would be in the cool of early morning. She gathered her nerve and walked through the atrium to the door of the screened porch. "Grandfather Raymond? Are you there?" When there was no answer, she knocked, staccato, on the aluminum door.

Dora came, white streaks on a strawberry apron. "Tally Carver!" She spoke loudly, so Raymond would hear. "How nice to see you again. Raymond is just finishing his supper. We eat early, so I can get on home. Come on in, Tally." She unhooked the screen door and leaned to speak softly to the young woman, who looked so different from the last time she was here.

"Hope this isn't bad news. Joshua didn't come to lunch Sunday. I'll say a prayer."

Dora led the way into the dining room, where Tally had to do all the required turning down of an extra plate, a drink, some dessert? She finally buttered one of Raymond's cooling corn biscuits and nibbled at it. When polite chatter ended, Tally found herself impaled on the point of Grandfather Raymond's gaze, and she realized he had not yet said a word.

"I'll just clear the last of these condiments," Dora said, "and go on home now. Tally, will you put Raymond's cup and spoon in the dishwasher before you go?" Zip, buzz, and the aging, nosy, loving woman was gone.

"I'll go to the porch now, *Wy-no-na*," he said, raising himself with the aid of a gnarled walking stick. "The honeysuckle hangs heavy and sooths my spirit. You bring my tea." Raymond Wooden Headdress struggled with the revolver and holster hanging on his chair, placed it on his shoulder. Tally followed his halting progress to the spot he commandeered on the front porch and sat on a lower stool in front of him. "Got to keep moving, *Wy-no-na*. Good for the legs. Good for the whole man." He sat in meditation, tea mug untouched. Tally welcomed the quiet and waited for him to speak.

"My grandson did not come for lunch Sunday. I have heated the rocks each morning, yet he does not come. His *chos-kay* is now cleared of all wrongdoing, yes? Still, he stays away, and you are here. You seek advice about the proud man, my grandson."

Tally dug into the briefcase at her side. "Actually, Grandfather Raymond, I need to return the gift. Your wife's brooch. Joshua has…well…left me, I guess. I don't understand, and—"

"You had not shared the pallet when you were here together, I think. Yet your love for one another shone for all to see. I cannot believe he has left you. A discord, perhaps. Harmony must be practiced, *Wy-no-na*."

"It's about red and white, I think, Grandfather. Maybe a little about Mr. Marsden, who lives in my building. Now it's four days, and his last words were 'forget about it.' So I must try to forget about it."

Raymond did not immediately respond. His leathery face tested the air and filled his lungs with honeysuckle. His words were measured and careful when he spoke, and his all-knowing eyes exuded the wisdom of his ninety-three years.

"You could do that. It might even be easier, at first. Yes, you could do that."

Tally absently polished the petals of the daisy pin with the paper that surrounded it and waited for the old man to resume speaking. His eyes closed, and she thought he might have nodded off. "But you want me to do something else?"

Raymond Wooden Headdress squared his shoulders, for he had decided to tell the story. "My Cecelia and I were not yet blessed with Joshua's mother when I went with the men on a Saturday. We broke some horses and drank a lot of whiskey, and there were two women in Scobey who took Indians. They left me there, sitting up beside the building of the women, like the drunk Indian I was.

"She would know immediately, and I did not go home. I went to the ranch, where we broke the horses and stayed in the bunkhouse and broke more horses in the dust and the August heat and sweated the whiskey from my body. She came, driving alone in a rickety, borrowed Model-A with our child large in her. She was so brave, my Cecelia.

"'The white man's war is over,' she said. 'Ours will not begin. You will come home now, and we will forget the one sour note you piped in the entire song of our life together.' And I went with her—home. And honored her all of my life."

Tally wept without ceasing. Great courses of tears washed her cheeks, and she tried to hush her sobs. Raymond leaned to place a hand on each of her shoulders.

"Go to him, child. Tell him there is no war. Tell him your love will insulate him, and his love will protect you, for all the days of your lives. Trample his false pride once and for all. Will you let your true love pipe past your window and be gone forever because one note was sour?" He leaned back and sucked at the dregs of the tea in his mug.

Sniffling, Tally nodded her head. "I have to try, don't I? I can't just let him stay away without—you know, he said we could talk about anything. Oh, Grandfather, thanks for the story." She had gathered her body to stand, when

Raymond took the brooch from her hand and stripped it of its wrapping.

"Lean down here, Tally Carver." His shaky hands pinned the black and diamond daisies on her left lapel. "Feel the spirit of Cecelia." Tally wept again.

"And don't cry!" Raymond scolded her. "Our clan is not drawn to weeping women! Now," he went on, "my grandson is surely at Red Bottom, for his *chos-kay* and *wy-no-na* will be involved in the feast that's going on right now. You will want to find him in mid-afternoon tomorrow. I would be in prayer tonight, child. I would pray for relief from the bondage of self, and for a life that honors my love.

"That's what I would do," he concluded, handing over his mug and spoon and closing his eyes again. Dismissal was obvious. Tally was to go. On the return trip from the dishwasher, she breathed her thanks and was not sure he heard. She patted Cecelia's pin for courage and faith and strolled down the walk, luxuriating in the sweet fragrance there.

Fluorescent hummingbirds were busy at the honeysuckle, darting sips that would become their fuel for the chill night ahead. Redheaded and green-backed, they buzzed at her hair, but did not flit far from their blossoms. Sundown would come too soon. She watched them from the car for a moment. Every day, the tiny birds operated on the faith that there would be enough nectar to get through the night. I could learn something from hummingbirds, she mused, as she started the Oldsmobile's engine.

Tally crisscrossed the streets of Poplar as she had done the first day her car arrived there. It was not so brown and dusty as then; the weekend thunderstorm had released clumps and cascades of greenery in corners and crevices everywhere.

Snow-on-the-mountain tumbled over low fences and rock gardens throughout the town, its tiny white flowers so profuse that no stem or blue-green leaf showed beneath them. Poplar's well-tended yards boasted only a rare gardener tonight. The feast was over, the Camping Day youth powwow was beginning, and Poplar's Assiniboine population and many of its Sioux were on the outskirts of Frazer at the Red Bottom celebration.

The determined young woman clutched at Cecelia's brooch again as she turned the car toward home. It had been a day of tough decisions. I like it here. I like the town, the people, my work. I will stay, no matter what. She was hungry. Raymond's private stock biscuit had caused her stomach to complain of neglect, and her mind was in the refrigerator and building a sandwich before she had the apartment door unlocked.

Showered and wrapped in her fuzzy robe, French doors open, she absently watched "Working Girl" on VCR. The Melanie Griffith/Harrison Ford/Sigourney Weaver movie had been a favorite of hers since she was a high school student aspiring to great things after college. The confrontation and showdown in the elevator was just beginning when a knock sounded at the door.

I swear, she thought. If that is Gerry Marsden, I will scream at him in no uncertain terms. On the way to the door, she thought to ask herself why she no longer thought it might be Joshua. She tied her belt robe tighter, straightened the sagging towel on her wet hair and opened the door.

James-Dale stood there in the burgeoning dusk, a colorful bundle that could only be her star quilt in his outstretched hands. She wanted to peer beyond him, and didn't. Shock at his visit was obvious from her demeanor. Joshua's son was here, and with her quilt.

"James-Dale! Come in, come in." The happiness she felt at seeing him lilted out in her voice. "Could that be my star quilt that your Aunt Rosie gave me?"

He was uncomfortable, but not the same sullen boy he had been on movie night. His tongue raced his brain. "It is, and it's going to have to be cleaned, we think, and Grandma told me to tell you the cleaners in Wolf Point is better than Glasgow for the quilts, and when it gets older you can wash it and—"

"Whoa! Whoa down, James-Dale! I only caught about a third of that. Let's start over." She smiled and took the quilt from him. "Thank you for coming to my home, James-Dale Smith," she said. "Won't you come in and sit? Have a cold drink?"

"Really, Tally, thanks. Aunt Christy is waiting for me down below. Boy, will I be glad when I can drive next year!" Boyish pride prevailed. "I already know how, just no license."

"Can I ask how you got my quilt back? This is obviously the same one." She looked at it carefully, and then the boy pointed to the little crocheted rose in an unobtrusive corner. A rose for Rosie, of course. She hadn't noticed that before.

She remained in the kitchen with her beloved's son, standing and listening. "It's such a long story, Tally. Everybody on the rez knows that Aaron Painted Rock is the crack dealer. My dad is friends with his oldest brother, and Dad got Johnny to go to Aaron to get your stuff. 'Or else,' my dad said, and he meant it!"

James-Dale tossed his long, black hair as his fierce Indian eyes flashed, and his slender chest swelled. "When my dad says it, he flat means it, and everybody knows that. So Johnny brought the quilt to my house."

Tears started, and Tally buried her face in the fabric. She jerked away from it immediately. "Oh, it will surely need cleaning, won't it? Smells like a tavern or something. Lots of cigarette smoke. Anyway, I'm grateful to have it back. Thanks so very much."

"My dad says you didn't think for a minute it was me, Tally. That was way cool, how you made them get the real guy." Head down, he now counted the cracks in the tile of the kitchen floor as he slowly finished his story. "I finally had to tell him where I was. Some guys and I were goofing off too much on the Red Bottom campgrounds. The Frazer marshal brought us ten miles from Poplar and made us walk home. I am grounded 'til the end of July except for family stuff." He didn't seem sorry.

When he turned to go, he remembered what else he wanted to tell her. "Oh, Johnny Painted Rock is sorry about your diamond, Tally. Aaron will say he never had it should anyone ask him, but the truth is, it is gone to Billings already. That's why we only got the quilt."

"Stand there while I put on some sweats, James-Dale. I'll walk you down," and she ran to the bedroom, yelling to keep him there. "The quilt is the only important thing, James-Dale. If I had to make a choice, I would have chosen it. Don't worry another minute about the ring. What's more, insurance will pay a little something on the jewelry!" Hurriedly dressed, she came from the hallway, running her hands through her heavy, damp hair.

His hand was on the door, and his words were so subdued she strained to hear. "Anyway, Tally, family stuff could be popcorn night again. If you'd invite us, I mean. I could get out of the house and stuff." He was unable to go further and scuffed at the floor, but her heart sang at his off-handed inclusion of her in the family.

Guess I should get him to talk to his father! Either they don't communicate, or Joshua is also hoping against hope.

The summer solstice was upon Montana, and the outside lights winked on just as Tally followed the boy down the steps. Even then, it was nearly light enough to read. Her watch said it was 9:30. The boy quick-stepped to the car, and her words followed him. "How come you guys aren't at the Youth Powwow?"

Then she was there, leaning toward the passenger window, open against the day's heat and humidity. "Hi, Christy. Thanks for bringing him and my quilt."

James-Dale said, "We were, but my dad wanted me to bring your quilt before you might be gone to bed."

Christy said, "We were, but—" and stopped. Her nephew had said all there was to say about Red Bottom Days. She looked at Tally with the same almond eyes that had shown so much concern in Joshua's living room. When Tally said nothing more, Christy started the engine on her Tercel.

Tally could not just let her go. "Christy. You've been so… fine. So fine, about coming out to get Joshua and caring about my situation. I thank you." She stood away from the car, and it began to pull away from the curb. And stopped.

"Come here," Christy motioned to the lovely white woman in the navy blue sweats, whose loose hair was an apricot halo against the dying sun. "I have to tell you," she whispered through the driver's window and fiddled with the gearshift. "I was jealous. Afraid no one will ever love me like he loves you. Now, I just want him to be happy." Christy looked up at Joshua's lover. "He's sure miserable right now, Tally." She engaged the gear and drove away slowly, watching the other woman in the side view mirror until she turned the corner out of sight.

Chapter Fifteen

Her sleep was untroubled. She clutched, still, the braid of sweet grass she had rested her head upon as she prayed at the side of her bed. "I'm not too good at this, Sir," she had said. "I will practice. And practice. Relieve me of whatever it was— self-righteousness—and put me on a path to be worthy of love. I will try to do Your will. Thank you." She had felt a little foolish when she knelt, and found herself filled with a sweet warmth when she rose. Tally slept immediately, and dreamed not.

Friday was payday and play day. The office basics barely handled, twelve noon arrived, and all but Tammy Runsbelow raced from the office to attend or participate in Red Bottom Days. Tammy had a special little sorting project, while Tally and Bob worked together in the conference room. They were crosschecking numbers for the reports to the Council on July 11. When the June quarter closed, they'd just drop in the last ten days of June and would be prepared and on time.

"It will be the first time in two years we didn't just give them an estimate!" Bob was ecstatic. "Tally, I am overjoyed to be working with you and for you!"

"Okay," she said, laughing. "It's two-thirty. You've sweet-talked me enough. Go on home. We're done here, anyway."

She sent Tammy home at 4:00, and drove straight to Joshua's trailer on the Poplar River.

It wasn't much more than a creek, Joshua had told her, most of the year. Spring runoff caused it to flow fast and high, as it did right now. She drove slowly above the rushing water, safe on the road he'd carved out with his own hands, and inhaled the green river scent. As she rounded the last small bend, she took a deep breath and patted the black and diamond daisies at her throat.

Marsden's Cadillac was in the clearing beside Joshua's flatbed. Its passenger door hung open. Engineer did not come to greet her when she went to the trailer door and, when she knocked, there was no answer. Panic leaped in her throat. She clutched Cecelia's brooch for strength and calm.

"I'll sit here on the step," Tally announced to the clearing, "and wait for five minutes before I go looking for—anything." Resolutely, she looked at her watch, and then at her surroundings.

Everything was so green! Out there, beyond the gravel, it had been almost brown last weekend, with verdant stalks struggling to overcome winter's debris once again. Now it was lush, smelling of earth and life and the sun's love for Montana. She allowed the warmth to lull her senses for some minutes and lost herself in the remembrance of Joshua's mouth on hers.

Voices. There were voices, farther upriver and growing closer. Tally leaped from her reverie and circled the living room end of the trailer. Her subconscious recorded a derrick contraption on her left and behind it. She was trying not to be in shock over what she saw coming up the grassy bank.

It was a group. A carefree group. Joshua, Gerry, Engineer, Mazurka. Joshua, denim shirt flapping open over his bronze chest, was leading Mazurka from an upriver grazing area. Gerry Marsden's shirtsleeves were high on his arms, his tie askew on his shirtfront, and those were probably grass stains on the knees of his smooth Dockers. Engineer bounded happily in and out of the tall grass while the two men laughed and conversed. Until they saw her, that is. Then, silence reigned.

She was a sight to silence anyone. Dressed for sentimental reasons in the riding skirt and tall, soft boots, her high-breasted body challenged the two men as they approached her. Flawless skin echoed the glow of her hair in the western sun, and Joshua knew the scent of her long before he drew close. He noted his grandmother's brooch. Tally had come for him, he knew. Grandfathers, he prayed, make me worthy.

Marsden didn't speak, which amazed her as she stood in calm silence. Joshua did, in the soft, firm voice that set his words in stone. "Gerry has made his amends to me and mine, Tally. It is well that we forget the hard occurrences of the days past. I am glad you are here."

Gerry was lighthearted. "Thanks for showing me your place, Joshua. I'll be getting on home now, and probably see you at the celebration tomorrow." He took small, measured paces to stand directly in front of the woman who had turned his life upside down just yesterday, and took both her hands in his.

"Tally, I am indebted to you. I believe I have new eyes, thanks to your prodding of my conscience. Joshua knows I meant nothing personal, and I hope you know, too."

She nodded her head at him, and he released her hands reluctantly.

"Sure is a beautiful place," he sighed. "I wish you guys all the best in the world. Not hard to imagine you'd get it all, out here." He crunched gravel as he crossed the clearing. "Look here! I left the car door open, worried about the darn dog when I raced him to the trailer. Hey, Engineer!" The shepherd dashed to do some restrained frolicking while the new friend got in and started his engine. Gerry craned his neck and waved from his window all the way around the first bend.

Her sweetheart drank in the sight of her, a stone's toss across the clearing. She was tall and proud and, yes, determined. Now, she did not wait for him to speak.

"This war is over, Joshua Dale Smith, and we have a date for Red Bottom Days. You said, of course, we would go. You're an honorable man. Of course, we will go?"

"Well, yes, of course, Tally," he stammered, crestfallen. "Tonight or tomorrow? Or both?"

"Tomorrow, I think, Joshua. Take tonight to decide if you want your true love to pass by your window because of one sour note whistled. To ponder on whether people like Blue Cloud Ransome just got lucky in marriage, or whether unselfish love for one another had something to do with it. And, Joshua," she flaunted her body in his direction, "to also think about us not being together for the rest of our lives."

"Oh, Tally, I'm so sorry. I'll spend the rest of my worthless life trying to make it up to—"

She interrupted him. "Not so fast. I want you to think it over. You were right in the first place. It's too important to be carried away with sweet kisses, and then think we owe one another something. I'm a forever woman, Joshua. Forever, as in babies and six-bedroom houses. Talk to me about forever tomorrow at noon. Or don't. But, remember, it's going to be for all time."

Tally had to fight to keep from clutching at Cecelia's daisies while she blurted her impassioned ultimatum. The look that bespoke a century of sorrow was once again on his face. A meadowlark called on the prairie beyond, and she nearly broke down with the longing to hold him.

"Tomorrow at one o'clock," she finished resolutely, "I'm going to eat Indian tacos at Red Bottom Days. For lunch. I hope you'll be buying them." She turned to her car and confused the dog. Engineer looked from Tally to his master and back again, finally trotting over to his hideout under the trailer. She waved, as Gerry had, all the way to the first bend.

Joshua looked down the river long after the sound of Tally's car had retreated from his home site. Shaking his head harshly, he hurried to give Mazurka her nightly treat and to put some special jerked beef in Engineer's bowl. Immersed in silence, he went into his home, ran a damp washcloth over his face and arms, snapped his shirt, and tucked it in. Fifteen minutes after Tally had disappeared down his road, he was roaring after her in the Jeep.

He stood on Jo Ellen's porch. "Kids at Frazer, Jo Ellen?" When he learned that Christy would bring them home after the night's dancing, he stepped into her living room, breathing deeply of the fresh, crisp cotton smell of the quilt pieces she stitched.

"I may be going after her, Mother Red Leggins," he spoke formally to his elder. It was not necessary to elaborate on who "her" was. "First, I'll be in prayer over it. Then, if it is to be, I'll bring her and pick up the kids by 12:30 tomorrow, and we'll have lunch on the grounds up there. Tell James-Dale and Ellen that it's very important to me that they go to the celebration with me tomorrow noon. One way or the other." This last he spoke softly, already praying.

Jo Ellen raised her bulk from her easy chair, thumbing the mute button on the TV's remote control and cutting off Judge Judy in mid-pronouncement. In a rare display of affection, she wrapped her short arms around him as far as they would go and raised her dark cheek in invitation. He leaned down and laid his face against hers.

The aging widow spoke softly. "Go with love, my son. In the end, it's all you have." Shaking that nonsense from her thoughts, Jo Ellen stalked back to her chair, waving a hand behind her to dismiss him and to hide the lost tears that threatened. Once again, she stitched and did not hear the black-robed harangue from the television screen.

At the other end of Poplar, his grandfather was at the dinner table. Dora bustled about. "No, he don't want food, woman! Sit here and stop fussing. Grandson, the rocks are hot. I have heated them all day."

"May I speak with you first, Grandfather?"

"No, grandson, you may not. Hurry to be in prayer, before your life passes you by." Raymond closed his eyes and pretended to sleep. Chastened, Joshua hurried to the sweat lodge.

Tally busied herself around the apartment Friday afternoon and evening. She dusted and vacuumed every corner, and ran up and down to the laundry room. Outside, on the staircase, she lifted her head into the breeze and tasted the scent of green things. The weed field Joshua and the kids had cleaned and mowed was dotted with red and yellow wildflowers. A large clay dish of purple petunias and speckled golden marigolds sat outside Candy St. Alban's front door. I still have not met little Jerome, she thought as she admired the potted blooms. They're not home again. Probably at the powwow.

The little Swiss clock had barely finished chiming seven o'clock when the phone rang. "Tally, it's Joshua. I'm at the Texaco."

She resisted the impulse to ask if he was buying anything. "Joshua, I thought we were going to see each other tomorrow noon. This is a—"

"Tally Jo, I can't come tomorrow, and I need to see your face about it. I'll be there in five minutes, okay?"

She looked at the receiver, amazed and proud and fearful. He hadn't even really said goodbye, and he sounded like a man who finally knew what he wanted. She wished she knew what it was, but "can't come tomorrow" sounded ominous. I won't borrow trouble. I'll just wait. He might have to work. Tally fluffed at her hair with her right hand as she opened the kitchen door. Then she seated herself on the far end of the couch where she had a direct view of the screen door. Her eyes were blue-gray and quiet, waiting.

He rapped before he saw her through the screen and waited to hear, "Come in!" before he entered. Still wet, his blue-black hair was again in the thong-wrapped ponytail, and soft leather moccasins had replaced his boots. He wore an unusual cotton shirt pulled over his jeans, pale blue and without buttons. Narrow satin ribbons of different lengths and colors hung from its front yoke and fluttered as he strode toward her.

Joshua felt her observation of his powwow garb, and stopped short. He stretched his body up and bent it over in a question mark. His feet began a peculiar one-two, one-two dance rhythm, and he crouched lower and lower as he danced toward her. As he approached her, the imaginary staff in his right hand kept time to the drums she could almost hear. She was sorry when he reached her seated form, ended his dance with two mighty thumps of the unseen staff and straightened his body.

"It's the sneak-up dance, Tally darlin'. I have sneaked up on you from the front 'cause I am a really brave brave!" His white teeth flashed in his dark face, and passion beamed from his black eyes. Tally exhaled the breath she had been holding all week. "We have to go to the powwow now, Tally. Do you have a shawl?" He slumped into the recliner, as if the dance had exhausted him.

"Shawl? Er...I have a stole. Square, with a fringe."

"That's a shawl out here, baby!" His grin told her the vulgar delivery was intentional. "We don't want to miss the final dancing. Would you put on your riding skirt and boots and bring your shawl?" Joshua was deliberately animated, intent on keeping his desire for her in check.

Tally sat, torn between his wardrobe suggestion and trying to insert some sanity into the moment. Her left brain went to work and sanity won. "Joshua, we have so much talking to do. Why can't we go tomorrow as we planned?"

"I have to stay on the place tomorrow, Tally. C'mon, get dressed, and I'll tell you everything in the Jeep. Remember how far it is to Frazer? We're burnin' daylight!" He pulled her to her feet.

She was shocked at his physical response to the touch of her hands. While she deliberated falling into his arms, he spun her around quickly and pushed her bottom in the direction of the bedroom hallway.

"I'll get a couple cans of tea," he said. "Hurry, now."

She hurried, and soon they were both on the staircase, where Joshua stroked his forehead with icy aluminum.

Fragrance assailed her nostrils again as they descended the stairs to the Jeep. "Oh, my," she exclaimed. "That new, green smell is so luscious. It just happened all of a sudden."

"It's *Waxbeashmawi*," he replied. "Full Leaf Moon, in the Assiniboine language. The Sioux call it *Wipasuka Sapa Wi*, which roughly translates to Juneberries Black Moon. It seems to come upon us exactly at the time of Red Bottom Days."

"*Wax be ash ma wi*," she parroted. "I'm learning a lot of Assiniboine. *Chos kay. Wy no na*, I figured out myself. Means 'daughter,' doesn't it? And now *Wax be ash ma wi*."

There was that sly grin again. "Yep. You know about half of what I do, already. Raymond and Cecelia, they were sent away to Indian school, where the missionaries tried to erase the Indian from the kids. They didn't talk it much until they were old, so my mother never learned."

He drove expertly, checking his rear and side view mirrors often and speaking to her in the mirror instead of taking his eyes from the road. He did that now, in an artificial voice that had to vie with the wind noise in the Jeep.

"I've got a pile of lumber coming tomorrow. Lucky to get it at all, much less on a Saturday. I have to meet them on the highway and guide the load in, and who knows for sure when they'll get there? Sometime after twelve noon, is all they'll guarantee. Then I have to get it tarped. It's $54,000 worth, for framing the house. Don't want it to get wet. You can go to Frazer with James-Dale and Ellen, if you want to. Take them, I mean. Tomorrow."

Speechless lasted only a moment. "Fifty-four thousand dollars? Fifty-four thousand? Joshua, I don't understand.

Never mind you're building the house before you recapture the horse that escaped, or I haven't even said for sure I wanted to be recaptured—" She giggled, unable to be stern in the presence of his loving profile, and capitulated. "Well, okay. You love me. I love you. You'll tell me sometime soon. So be it. But, Joshua, do you have fifty-four thousand dollars?"

He was inscrutable again, sly innocence on his face as he took his eyes from the road for an instant. "Well, Tally, I thought you probably did. And I thought I should get started on the house right away. A roof over all those babies' heads and such."

A tremor of joy, of anticipation ran through her even as her accountant's head scanned its personal balance sheet. She'd have to cash her C.D., but it would be worth it. "Well, yes, I do, but we're going to have to talk about making mutual decisions, Joshua. Partners talk to each other. Remember, you're the one who said that?"

He nodded as if properly chastened. "Okay, I've got two plans for houses that fit against that little hillside beyond the lean-to. You can pick the one you want. And everything inside, of course." They drove another fifteen minutes in silence, she already furnishing her own thirty-foot living room, while he watched her covertly in the mirror.

Another thought struck her fevered left brain. "Oh, Joshua. That was a well-drilling outfit I saw behind the trailer, wasn't it? You're getting the well now, too? How much is it?"

"No more than three thousand, honey. The water's there, and I'll do most of the work myself, putting up the pump house and all. They just have to drill to the water. They'll start again Monday, after Red Bottom Days." He was grinning now, watching her make computations in her head, but he said no more as they reached the edge of Red Bottom parking. The sound of many drums reverberated.

Chapter Sixteen

In single file, they edged through three hundred dusty cars to the area Tally had seen just two weeks ago. Joshua was right; she wouldn't have recognized it. There were at least twenty counter-fronted vendor tents in the cleared area beyond the makeshift parking lot. Memories of the carnival tents at the pony fair on Chincoteague rushed at Tally, sweet childhood memories that sparkled in her eyes. Even the smells were familiar. Popcorn and hamburgers, spices and chili permeated the air.

"Oh, Joshua, I'm hungry," she breathed, looking at the vendor's clearing. Thirty people were at various booths, and there was lots of room. She relaxed and prepared to enjoy an uncrowded spectacle, a wide-eyed tourist with a fringed, blue shawl over one arm.

"Let's see if the kids have eaten first, honey," Joshua began. "They're here someplace. James-Dale is not allowed to get out of Christy's or Ellen Joy's sight." The words had barely left his mouth when the drums stopped with a crash.

The split second of pure silence was shattered by what Tally could only call "war whoops," and the area they occupied was at once filled with noisy people of all sizes and shapes. Old and young, brown and white, they jostled and cavorted as they pushed their way to the vendor of their choice.

Humanity surrounded her. The smell of sweat and whiskey was strong in the sun when a group of especially boisterous men pressed past her. Some Indian teenagers in feathers and buckskin whooped and whirled by, creating their own space. Tally took a deep breath and called on her reservoir of calm to subdue panic.

A grip of steel encircled her left elbow. Without words, Joshua guided her through a crowd that did not impede them as they passed. She discerned his nods of recognition to this person and that, but their measured progress did not halt. She gave herself up to the feel of him and the scent of the sweet grass emanating from his ribbon shirt, and her heart was full. Tears filled her darkening eyes in the certain knowledge that he knew her unspoken fear and was rescuing her.

He turned her, making a sharp corner around the last vendor tent. Two very young couples had escaped there and were stealing kisses before returning to the festivities. Joshua released her elbow and cupped her face in both his hands. "I will honor you and protect you all of my life, Tally Jo Carver," he articulated slowly. Without a glance at their audience, he sealed his vow with the lover's kiss she remembered.

"Now," he said, as he pulled away, "I'm going to get you an Indian taco. Spread that shawl on the ground right here and be here when I get back, okay?" The teenagers left the private area reluctantly. Their backward glances asked why these old folks had to sneak away to make out.

Amazing. Just amazing. He knows it's the crowd, not the people, and that I'm not afraid to sit back here by myself.

What a helpmate I'm acquiring! She sat on her pricey cashmere shawl, smiled at all who wandered by, and didn't recognize Joshua's kids for a moment.

"Dad's getting us fry bread tacos!" Ellen Joy shyly held out her hand to her father's sweetheart. "But we have to eat fast, because the Teen Traditional Dance finals are next." James-Dale elbowed his sister and nodded knowingly at Tally. He pantomimed a big, wet kiss. The pretty girl shoved him with an athletic forearm and warned him to shut up if he knew what was good for him.

"She's sweet on an Omaha!" James-Dale teased at his sister while protecting his face with his arms in near-fear. "An Omaha wasp!"

Tally was sure this was not the same kind of W.A.S.P. she'd worked with at the B.I.A., but didn't ask for an explanation. "Won't you share my shawl here?" she asked Ellen Joy, just as Joshua rounded the corner with a cardboard lid filled with paper-wrapped delicacies and several drinks.

"Hey, Dad," his daughter offered, "let me help you with that. Aunt Christy is keeping our seats, and we brought Grandma's chair for one of you. We better go back there and eat this, so we don't miss the start of the dancing. And you…" Ellen pointed with emphasis at her brother, "…you just shut up!"

And so it was that Tally found herself in the family group and heading toward the seating area.

Christy stood and held out her slender arm. "Tally. I am so glad you are here. Please, take my mother's chair, this one. She's not coming." Christy's voice was sincere and loving, and Tally reveled in its acceptance, seating herself with a teary smile.

With food in all hands, only James-Dale and Joshua remained standing. A camp stool next to Tally was empty. "Do
you want to sit, Dad?" His son was solicitous. Joshua glared
at the fifteen-year-old and did not speak. After a minute,
James-Dale hung his head and muttered, making himself a
place on the ground in front of his sister.

"What was that? I didn't hear you!" Joshua was terse. It
was obvious the boy wasn't getting off lightly for his Saturday night transgression.

"I said 'I guess any kid who can walk ten miles can sit
on the ground,' Dad. Please seat yourself, my elder." He was
not mocking. Announcement of the Men's Teen Traditional
Dance Finals cut short the exchange.

All eyes went to the brush-circled clearing and its arbors.
Sixteen boys in sizes from five to six feet and from seventy
pounds to two hundred seventy advanced into the near ring
in their finest regalia. Reds and blues on brown buckskin
predominated. A single drumbeat counted cadence as they
paraded counterclockwise. The youths were breathtaking.

Tally gasped and nearly choked on her final bite of Indian
taco. Informational films shown periodically at the Bureau of
Indian Affairs did not prepare her for the three-dimensional
immediacy of it as the drum quickened and the dance began. Two Assiniboine and one Sioux from Fort Peck were in
the finals, Joshua pointed out to her. They were resplendent
in turkey and eagle feather bustles and headdresses. Each
danced differently, yet all with that one-two step Joshua had
used to 'sneak up' on her earlier.

A good-looking boy in yellow and black drew her attention, both for his innovative dance and for Ellen Joy's obvious
interest in him. So this was the Omaha wasp? His regalia had

a bird's head in the middle of the bustle and another on the feathered staff with which he accentuated his movements. Each trip around the circle found this young warrior doing his own sneak-up in another portion of the trampled arena. His crouching body in its gleaming breastplate stalked an invisible enemy. The rapacious eyes on his bird staff seemed to screech, telling what the warrior would do when he overtook them. He was a story in dance, the young Omaha.

"Look at the great dancer in the yellow and black, Joshua," she said loudly into his ear. "Are those eagle heads?" She noted Ellen's interest in their conversation.

"No, dear white girl. Boys have hawks. Some of the Omaha men will have eagles. He is good, isn't he?" Joshua didn't look at his daughter, but Tally could tell he was aware of the infatuation.

The drums crashed and ended the dance. As before, thunderous silence reigned for a millisecond. Then the mob roared again toward the vendors and the parking area.

Joshua leaned close to her, put an arm around her shoulder, and shielded her from the crowd. He whispered in her ear and sent tingles to the soles of her feet. "Did you enjoy it, my darling? Do you want to stay for more, or—"

Joshua stiffened and stopped talking. A yellow and black apparition was sidling nonchalantly toward their group. Tally felt his fatherhood kicking in. Good, good, she thought. He'll protect the children, too. She looked up at a youth about James-Dale's age, stripped of his unique grace and beauty when the drums stopped. Just a boy in black and yellow regalia, now. And nervous.

"Hi, Matthew." Normally assertive, Ellen Joy spoke softly and looked at him with downcast eyes. "This is my dad and his girlfriend. Joshua Smith, Tally Carver, this is Matthew Wolf. He's from Nebraska." The boy didn't quite scuff, but looked around uncomfortably as if for an ally of his own. Joshua put out his hand.

"Good job, good dance, Matthew," Joshua praised.

"Oh, yes!" Ellen chimed in. "You'll surely win!"

He was resolved. "No, I don't think so. Sometimes I do, but the local kid in the red and blue was very good. And it is their party, after all. I'll be glad to take second." He took his eyes from Ellen long enough to notice Tally's interest in his regalia. He stepped closer so she could put a hand on his chalk shiny breastplate, a double ladder from throat to waist. Narrow rawhide thongs tied it around his body.

"It's bird bones, ma'am. Lots of them. People think they are light, but they sure get heavy after a whole day in them! And the yellow and black are for west and north, life and death. Here, in the bustle…" he pointed to the course of feathers at his young boy's buttocks "…is the trail of the warrior's life. Mine is not too long. Yet." He stood tall, and a glimpse of the man he was to be emerged. It disappeared the moment he eyed Ellen Joy again. "Um, Ellen. Want to go for a cold drink?"

She looked at Christy, and then at her dad, who leaped at the opportunity to do some fathering. "Yep, why don't you kids all go get something. Here." He took folding money from the right-hand pocket of his jeans, separated some and gave the rest over to James-Dale. "Nice to have met you, Matthew." Joshua shook the boy's hand again. "You should win. Good luck."

Joshua walked a step with them and patted James-Dale heavily on the shoulder as the trio went to the vendors. Don't

let your sister out of your sight, was his unspoken instruction. When he turned back, Christy and Tally were chatting
easily about the dancers, like the sisters they would be.

Oh, Grandfathers, thank you. He sat on his stool, eyes
closed, for a prayerful minute. Then he spoke to the women.
"Christy, do you have to go to the bathroom or something? I
have a personal thing here that just can't wait."

His sister-in-law laughed out loud and shook her head at
the insanities of couples in love. Brushing fry bread crumbs
from her lap, she rose and wandered off. "I'll be back before
the Women's Jingle starts," she warned. Indeed, people were
thronging back to their seating areas already.

"Tally, honey. This is my last confession. Well, two con-
fessions. I've not been quite honest." Her face didn't change,
for she didn't care. He would honor her from this time forward, she knew.

"Out with it! Out with everything, right now," she answered serenely. "Let's not waste any more precious moments
of our lives." She fussed with black daisies and smiled.

He faced her, holding both her hands. "The present? The
one Raymond gave me that Sunday? He split up the last oil
money three ways a long time ago. Says it flowed under all
our land, mine and Rosie's, even if it was drilled only on his.
He didn't give me mine at the time." Joshua was caressing
the tops of her hands with his big thumbs, reflecting on the
wisdom of his grandfather. "Good thing," he said simply. "It
would have killed me then."

She didn't move, luxuriating in the sensual movement
of his thumbs on her soft hands, afraid he'd stop. She didn't
know what to say. Oil? That was a lot of money, probably.

"So," he went on, "with interest all these years, I now have
$867,943.22 in the bank. Tax-free, you know, since it came

from the land. You don't really have to pay for the lumber or the well, sweetheart. In fact, you're going to be a well-to-do wife. And mother."

He continued to make love to her hands, proud of his ability to ignite the passion in her eyes.

"Well, that's real nice, Mr. Smith. You're probably marrying me because I'm a proven money-manager! Well, okay, that's okay. What's the other thing you want to confess?"

Christy was wending her way through the seated revelers and would be upon them in a minute. He left her hands reluctantly and leaned back on his stool with a sensuous smile. As his sister-in-law seated herself and pretended interest in something far, far away, he put his right arm around Tally's shoulder and drew her ear to his whispering mouth.

"I don't really want to stay for more, Tally Jo. I've been to the Texaco and the Mini-Mart twice already, and I think Mazurka and Engineer are missing you. Us."

Her eyes closed as his breath kissed her neck, and her nipples grew rigid. She was silent, loving him.

"Ah, Christy? Keep an eye on that young Omaha warrior, won't you? I'm going to take Tally here out where the sweet grass grows." He lifted his beloved to her feet, the blue shawl sliding from her lap.

"It's the season for it," Christy chuckled. "It's sweet grass season, all right."

Tally pretended concern. "Why did I bring my shawl, Joshua? I thought we were going to dance, together." She arranged it around her shoulders and under her apricot hair, shuffling her feet in an approximation of the one-two step she'd been observing.

"Tonight, it's my second favorite thing, Miz Carver," he quipped, his deep eyes promising joy heaped upon delight.

"We'll dance tomorrow night. C'mon, we're burnin' day-light."

He took her elbow firmly, and guided her through the crowd to the parking lot as if it were his life's work. Then, hand in hand, they went to the Jeep and on to the swift green river, there to properly begin forever.

Only a meadowlark and a happy dog heard her inno-cent question as he swept her through the silver trailer's door. "What's your first favorite thing tonight, Joshua Dale Smith?"

LaVergne, TN USA
22 September 2009
158630LV00001B/17/P